The Tiger's Heart

Alaskan Tigers: Book Two

Marissa Dobson

Published by Sunshine Press

Printed in the United States of America

ISBN-13: 978-0-9886684-2-3

DEDICATION

To my husband, Thomas who spent many hours listening to my ideas for the Alaskan Tigers series.

To my sister Jenifer who loves tigers as much as I do. She inspired me to write the Alaskan Tigers.

Contents

Chapter One

Papers and maps cluttered the table. The search for Pierce filled every hour. The flow of viable information trickled. They had men following up leads, searching known vacations spots for the rogue and his gang. Most of the leads turned out to be dead ends, but they couldn't afford to leave any stone unturned. The rogues could not get away.

The situation ate away at Raja's gut, while frustration showed on Ty's face. They seemed no closer to finding Pierce, yet they sensed his men were in the mountains watching them. His assassin teams stalked the area, waiting for them. Rarely did anyone leave the compound, especially not the women and children—not with the danger surrounding them.

"Raja, stop pacing. You're going to wear a hole in my favorite rug," Ty's mate Tabitha teased. She watched him over her coffee mug as he paced the study.

He smiled, unable to help it. Tabitha had a way of lightening the mood. *When I find my mate I hope she is able to make me smile the way Tabitha can. This woman has been through so much, yet she still is more concerned about the people around her than herself.*

"You know I'm good for another one." He couldn't sit still. The hairs on the back of his neck stood at attention. Something wasn't right. Something was about to break; he could feel it in his soul. Pierce would make a move before long, but what would that move be?

"Leo and Connor arrived in California and are on their way to locate Pierce's sister. It's extremely unlikely that he's there, but maybe she'll be able to tell us something." He ran his hand over the windowsill. Outside looked like a winter wonderland. Thick, white snow covered everything and the weather reports forecasted more snow over the next few days.

"Keep me apprised of the situation. I want them back within seventy-two hours, or we send in another team. We don't have the time to waste on this." Ty sat reading the reports from the teams trying to track Pierce and his clan. Teams were all over the country, yet no one had seen hide or hair of the rogues. Pierce knew they were searching for him, but they didn't expect him to run and hide. Maybe the fact that his days were numbered, for the murder and attacks on other tiger shifters, had him scared.

Raja nodded, still gazing out the window.

"I need to go speak with some of the guards. Raja, could you look after Tabby until I get back? I don't want to leave her alone in case there's another attack."

"Sure."

"Thank you." Ty rose, kissing his mate's cheek. "I shouldn't be long, love."

Once they were alone Raja heard Tabitha's chair push back from the table, and the sound of her approach in sock-covered feet.

"Raja, are you okay?" She laid her hand on his back, offering comfort. Unfortunately, it only worked on a mate, but the caring gesture touched him.

"I'm fine. You have enough to worry about. Don't concern yourself with me." If he could hear the uncertainty in his voice—no doubt she could.

"I don't believe you. If you ever need to talk, I'm here. It will go no further than us."

"Mates don't keep things from each other." Reservation thickened his voice.

"To help a friend in need I would do what needs to be done. Raja, I haven't known you very long, but I consider you a part of my family and can see your pain." She rubbed his back.

"Thank you, but everything is fine with me. It's you I'm worried about. I can feel something bad is coming." He wasn't being entirely honest. Something else bothered him, but he couldn't put his finger on it, let alone put it into words to tell his Queen.

"We'll get through it. We know Pierce is still out there and after me. He has a larger following than we guessed. I know it's your job as our Lieutenant to worry, but we'll survive."

The invisible ear bud allowing him contact with command central and the ground teams sprang to life. "Breach. We have a breach at the main gate. All available units respond."

"Shit. Where's Felix?" Raja turned to look at Tabitha.

"Ty gave him the morning off since we were meeting with you and wouldn't be leaving our quarters." Tabitha joined him at the window. "Go. I'll be fine."

"Like hell I will. You have to be protected." She had her own transmitter, allowing her to hear the same alerts, and fear spilled off her.

"Raja, stay where you are. Felix is on his way. I'm proceeding toward the main gate," Ty's order came through the transmitter.

"Be safe." Tabitha whispered.

"Tabitha, come away from the window. Everyone always forgets about the windows. You feel safe and secure inside the house, while the sharpshooter is waiting. Waiting for you to walk past the window." Raja could feel her reluctance, but his job was to keep her safe. Unlike the other guards, he hadn't vowed to protect her because she was their Alpha Female and Queen of the Tigers. No, his vow had been made to her mate. Ty who saved his ass more than once, and the best way to show his appreciation meant keeping her safe.

Chapter Two

Two knocks then a pause followed, but one more let him know Felix was on the other side of the door. Felix, Captain of Tabitha's guards, had a key to the quarters. The knock was a warning not to shoot him.

"Things are contained now." Felix said, sliding the lock back into place.

"What's the breach?"

"It sounds like a news crew."

"A what?" Tabitha questioned.

"A news crew, here to interview you."

Tabitha continued to stare at him as if he'd grown two heads.

"About your friend, Alice's, murder," he explained.

"Oh just what we need, news crews. Get rid of them. I want nothing to do with the whole mess."

"Ty's working on it. He explained that this is private property and they have no right to step foot on it. He'll get rid of them. In the meantime, sit tight."

News crews, who would have guessed? Raja chuckled to himself as he watched the exchange.

A roar shook the walls, echoing in the small space, and jerking him out of his amusement. "Tabitha, calm yourself. Your body isn't ready for this yet. Don't force it." The energy she radiated would make anyone in the room shift if they weren't careful. It vibrated along his skin, prickling every nerve.

"Ty, we need you back here. Now!" Raja hollered hitting the button on his ear transmitter. "Tabitha, Ty's on his way. Keep it together a few more minutes. Come on. You can do this." Roars echoed from the other side of the door, not every shifter was strong enough to fight the primal command. *I hope that they got the reporters to leave before they were able to see tigers roaming the grounds.*

"I'm on my way. Situation?" Ty's voice crackled through the ear bud.

Tabitha's growl nearly drowned out Raja's response. "Felix, unlock the door for Ty. We don't need anything slowing him down. He's the only one who can help her now." *How did I not see this coming?*

Raja didn't have time to question his choices now. He filed it away to examine later. Tabitha was his only priority. The first shift from human to tiger was painful and hard to control.

Ty came running through the door. They exchanged a brief look as Ty slid to a halt next to his mate, and Felix closed and locked the door behind him.

"Mate, you're not ready for this." She didn't seem to hear him. Her body shook. Roaring, she sent another wave of magic through the area.

"What the hell happened?" Ty eyed Raja.

"Take her anger from her. We can deal with why this happened later. If you don't stop her, this could kill her. I've seen this happen before. Help your mate."

Ty reached toward his mate, and pulled her into his arms. Growls vibrated the room, and pictures fell off the wall. His growls coursed with hers until they fell into an exhausted heap on the floor.

"What the hell happened?" Ty demanded in a voice hoarse from roaring.

"We're not really sure. I was explaining the situation at the main gate when she started..." Felix explained.

"It wasn't their fault." Tabitha spoke softly, her eyes closed, leaning heavily on her mate. "Felix mentioned the reporters and it brought back Alice's murder and everything that happened in Pittsburgh. My emotions got out of control, and I couldn't seem to do anything about it."

"Emotions are haywire when you go through the change." Ty kissed her forehead. "I'm going to put my mate to bed, and then we need to discuss the reporters and keeping them away from the compound. Felix, deal with the guards that shifted. Not all of them are strong enough to shift back, so find replacements." With that he rose, lifted his mate in his arms and stalked out of the room.

Marissa Dobson

Chapter Three

I should have been paying more attention to Tabitha's emotions. Allowing her to get that close to a shift without seeing it first was a fault I won't overlook again. Raja helped himself to another mug of coffee while he waited for Ty. Felix had left to deal with the guards.

Ty reentered the kitchen, shoulders slouched and steps dragging as if he should still be sleeping next to his mate. His body didn't glide as it normally did. Instead it seemed sluggish. He ran a hand through his long, dark hair and yawned. Raja poured another cup of coffee and slid it across the counter.

"Thanks."

Raja nodded and sipped his coffee. "You should be sleeping with her. I can deal with the reporters."

"I know you can. I have no doubts about that. But I needed to discuss something else with you." Ty took a drink of his coffee and raked his hand through his hair again.

His body tensed. His friend wasn't tired—something else weighed on his shoulders. Something that had him troubled.

"What's going on, Ty? We've always been straight with each other."

"I know I told you Tabitha's friend Alice was murdered. Well it seems as though the suspect is out on bond. The team I sent to keep an eye on him has been unable to locate him. He's disappeared."

"Bond? You're shitting me. He murdered two girls." Raja couldn't believe what he heard.

"Seems as though the justice system is fucked up. Jails are overcrowded. From what I can tell, it looks like someone pulled the right strings to get him out, and there's only one person I can think of who'd do that."

"She's safe as long as she's in the compound. We'll double her security to ensure that."

"It gets worse." Ty finished the last of his coffee. "It appears he has mob connections and may have teamed up with Pierce."

"How the hell did they find each other?" Tension thickened the air. This made things so much more dangerous. The sooner Tabitha could go through the change, the better. It would allow her to protect herself more if the situation grew worse.

"I'm guessing through the mob connection. We knew that Pierce had some limited connections there. The mob likes shifters on their payroll for extra protection."

"How much longer do you think until she goes through the change?"

"A week, two at most. She's close. Today proved it." Ty stood and put his coffee mug in the dishwasher.

"Are you going to tell her?"

"Sooner or later, yes. But not yet. She's too close, and I don't want to push her into the change too early."

It was the reasonable choice. "Then rest with her. You both need each other now. Let me fill Felix in, and we'll get a plan together and guard while you rest."

Ty nodded, slipping away to be with his mate.

Raja poured himself another coffee. The day promised to be long. The stress of not being able to make his mate safe ate at Ty. *If that's what it's like to be mated, I don't want any part of it.*

He sat in front of the laptop, trying to put his finger on Pierce's next move. *With all of this information, we should have some kind of lead.*

His cell phone dinged, letting him know that he had a new text message. *She agreed to meet us this evening. Will let you know how it goes.*

Leo was always a short and to the point sort of person. With a little luck, Pierce's sister would be willing to help. *Not that it will save his ass.* No way could they allow him to live after all of the people who died at his hand, and especially not for the attacks on Tabitha. Raja would kill him with his own hands if he had the chance.

* * *

Bethany danced around the hotel room. Coming to Alaska was a dream come true for her. Here for five days, she planned to see and do as much as she could jam into that time. When she won the trip she couldn't believe her luck—she didn't even remember entering the contest. She'd never won anything in her life.

She grabbed her cell from her purse and called her baby sister. When Jamie didn't answer, she left a message. "I can't believe Mom almost talked me out of coming. It's beautiful here. Mom's bad feelings are off. Nothing can go wrong. Tomorrow a day on the slopes, snowboarding. Tonight I plan to check out the nightclub the door attendant recommended. My cell reception is spotty, but I'll call you soon. Love ya, sis."

Tossing the phone on the bed, she glanced at the bedside clock. *Twenty minutes before the cab arrives. I have time to freshen up.*

* * *

"With Leo gone, I'd like Adam to be temporarily reassigned to Tabitha's guards. We need the expanded manpower," Felix said when they reconvened in Ty's office.

While Tabitha showered, they put together a quiet meeting to discuss the plans to double her guards without making her aware of any danger. Raja wasn't convinced that it was the best way to deal with the situation, but it was what Ty wanted.

"As long as he's teamed with a more experienced guard. He's used to guarding the grounds, not the Queen. If she has another episode like this afternoon, he won't stand a chance against the magic she exudes. We need someone who will still be able to fight if danger arises."

"Understood, Raja. I'll team him with Thomas."

"Very well then. We have the guards teamed up and scheduled. Remember, Tabitha doesn't need to know about this yet." Ty tapped the desk and the door opened.

Tabitha glared. Her face spelled out the truth—she'd overheard them and they were about to pay. "You don't want me to know about what?"

"It's nothing, darling." Ty rose from behind his desk to go to his mate.

"Nothing, my ass. You have been acting suspiciously all day, and I want to know what's up." Anger threaded in her voice as clear as an Alaskan Tiger's stripes.

Raja inched toward the door. The last place he wanted to be was in the middle of an argument between mates—especially his Alphas.

"I never took you as a coward, Raja." Her words startled him. Any chance of slipping out the door without her knowing vanished.

"My Queen, I'm not a coward, but it's not my place to get between two mates."

"Then tell me what's going on, since my mate would prefer to keep me in the dark." She fixed her irritation on him.

He could see Ty's position, but he was stuck. His Alphas wanted different things. "Tabitha, I think this is something that you need to discuss with him. I can only tell you, we're increasing your protection. We were meeting to discuss the guard schedule."

"Doubling my guards?"

Ty dropped onto his desktop in defeat. He didn't want to go up against his mate. "Tabby, things have become more dangerous. We're only trying to protect you."

"Keeping me in the dark isn't protecting me, Ty."

"With all due respect, she cannot afford the stress this is putting on her. Tell her." Raja murmured. It might not be his place, but he couldn't stand to see them both so torn up.

"Oh that will be less stressful for her, will it? Now you think you know what's better for my mate than I do!" Ty snapped.

"This is ridiculous. You can't keep it from me and we can't take our anger out on Raja. Don't shelter me. If I'm truly the Queen of the Tigers, then I have a right to know what the danger is."

"Leave. I'll fill her in." Ty growled.

Raja wasn't sure if Ty gave in out of defeat or because he realized they were right, but it didn't matter. Tabitha needed to know.

Chapter Four

Raja paced his quarters, unable to calm himself. He couldn't put his finger on it. There was something in the pit of his stomach that left him feeling ill. He checked the surveillance of the compound and everything appeared to be calm. *The calm before the storm. Oh, how I hope I'm wrong.*

Nothing to do, but wait—wait until the other shoe dropped. He'd never been good at waiting. He needed to run. Stripping off his clothes, he shifted.

* * *

The nightclub was like that of any other Bethany had been in before. The drinks flowed, music so loud she had to scream to talk and the dance floor crowded.

Partying and nightclubs weren't really her thing, but she'd promised her baby sister she would go. Jamie's words rang in her ears. *For once in your life, be wild. Let your hair down and do something you wouldn't. Go to a nightclub for me, dance and have a good time.*

"Can I buy you a drink?"

Turning on her bar stool, she found a man in jeans, and t-shirt with a cowboy hat riding low over his eyes standing behind her.

"Okay. I'll have a cola."

"A soda? Live on the wild side, darling. How about something stronger?

"Sorry. I don't drink the hard stuff," she said, shaking her head.

"I hate drinking alone, but I won't allow a lady to ruin my night." He motioned to the bartender.

His rudeness shocked her. She should have left then and there, but her mom taught her better. She allowed him to buy her a drink, so she'd finish it and then make her excuses. *Why did I ever let Jamie talk me into this?*

Life filled the club. Everyone laughed, having a good time it seemed, except her. She was completely out of her element.

"What brings you here tonight?" He leaned into her so he didn't have to shout.

"I promised my sister I would hit up a nightclub while here."

"You're not from here then?"

"No. I won this trip."

"Oh, you must be Bethany. I'm Josh, your ski instructor for tomorrow." He shook her hand.

"I changed that. I don't need an instructor. I decided to go snowboarding instead. But thank you for the drink." Finishing her soda, she rose. "I really must be going. It was a long trip, and I'm tired."

"Let me give you a ride back to the hotel. I have to go there anyway to pick up a few things."

"That's kind of you, but I already called a cab." She stood, sliding her purse over her shoulder.

"Come on." He grabbed her arm and pulled her toward the exit.

"You're hurting me." She tried to pull away from him, but his grip tightened.

"I'm going to hurt you if you don't come with me." He closed the distance between them, his voice a harsh whisper in her face. No one in the boisterous crowd seemed to see her distress.

Her heart beat feverishly, stomach rolling. *God help me, Mom was right. I should have listened.*

* * *

Raja ran until he exhausted his nervous energy. A run and a long, hot shower, and still he felt as if he was crawling to get out of his skin. His cell phone vibrated on the desk. *I hope this will be something to distract me.*

It was Leo.

"Raja." He answered and rose from his bed, listening.

"She'll only tell you and Ty and it has to be in person. What do you want us to do?"

"I'll speak with Ty and get back to you on that. There are some new threats where our Queen is concerned. I'm not sure he'll want a strange human within the compound. But if so, be ready to leave at a moment's notice."

"She doesn't seem like much of a threat and seems honestly concerned about her brother. We'll stand by for your word." It was late, but Ty would want to know immediately. He dialed his Alpha as soon as Leo hung up.

"Yes?" Ty's voice was heavy with sleep, and Tabitha murmured sleepily in the background.

"I'm sorry to bother you at this late hour. I heard from Leo, and I need to speak with you."

"Come over."

He'd never heard his Alpha sound so tired.

"I'll be right there." Raja hung up and slipped on a t-shirt. He didn't want to delay talking to Ty. Upon arriving at Ty's quarters, he was surprised to find Tabitha waiting in the living room as well. "My Queen, I didn't mean to disturb you."

"It's fine, Raja. I wouldn't be able to sleep without Ty anyway. What did you find out?"

Ty gave him permission with a slight nod.

"Jessica says she has information, but won't tell Leo and Connor what she knows until she meets with you. My guess would be she's trying to save her brother's ass."

Ty let out a deep sigh. "I would predict the same. I can't travel to speak with her in person, but I'll arrange a call tomorrow."

"She'll only do it in person. Leo asked about bringing her here. It's safer than the alternative." Raja disliked the idea, even if it was the only way to get the information from Jessica.

"I'm not sure it's safe, but it seems as if it is our only choice. Call Leo. I'll expect them tomorrow."

In the solitude of his quarters, Raja pulled his cell phone out.

"Leo. You're cleared to bring her here. We'll expect you tomorrow. But make it clear to her that if she brings danger to our clan, it will be her life on the line." He didn't wait for Leo to respond but ended the call. *Jessica could hold the key to finding Pierce, or she could be the key to our demise.*

Chapter Five

Sometime in the early morning hours, the sandman finally visited. It wasn't restful. Raja tossed and turned, strange and terrifying dreams plagued him. The turmoil from his mind was playing out in his dreams.

"Raja, you're needed in Ty's quarters." The ear bud that he kept in his ear at all times dragged him from his trouble sleep. When he was off duty, he set it to disturb only for an emergency.

He growled.

"We have a situation, and you're needed. Report immediately."

Situation? He didn't waste time changing. He grabbed his handgun from the nightstand and strapped his knife to his thigh before rushing down the short hall to Tabitha and Ty's area.

Felix opened the door. Behind him Ty comforted Tabitha. There didn't seem to be any immediate danger, but their Queen appeared distraught.

He stood waiting, knowing that Ty would fill him in.

"Tabby, there's no use in you being here for it again. Why don't you go into the study?" Ty said, trying to calm his mate.

"No. I'm fine."

"Tab…"

"If I'm to be Queen, I have to face even the worst things."

"You are Queen, but you don't have to do this. I won't argue with you. There's no time if we're going to save her."

Confusion filled him.

"Hit play and you won't have that look of confusion any longer." Ty nodded towards the laptop that sat on the table.

He stepped toward it and pushed the play button. A young girl filled the screen. Her eyes filled with terror and her blonde hair matted with dried blood. Her pleas, then her screams, filled the room as a man hit her over and over again.

"Bethany here will die unless you give up Tabitha Leigh. We tried to be civil about this and confront you directly. Now we'll kill innocent women until we have her. If you want the girl to live, drop Tabitha off in front of the Fairbanks International Airport at midnight. Once she's in our custody, you'll receive the girl's location. If you wish to play more games, she'll be the first of many dead women I leave in my wake." The terrified look in Bethany's eyes tour out Raja's heart. In all his years he witnessed some awful stuff and yet nothing affected him like the video did.

"Shit." He ran his gun-free hand over his face, feeling the slight stubble under his fingertips. "Did you put a trace on it?"

"Connor's working on it now." Ty nodded, his arm still wrapped tightly around Tabitha.

"I can't let her die because of me. If we can't find where this was sent from, I'll meet him."

"The hell you will, Tabitha!" Ty roared.

"That girl has nothing to do with this. She's innocent."

"Ty's right. You would be trading one life for another. There's no way we'll allow you to do that." No matter the cost he wouldn't allow his Queen to risk herself but he couldn't get the image of the girl out of his mind. Something about her called to him and he wanted to find her.

"Raja, I wasn't asking permission. I won't let her die in my place. She probably has a family that would miss her."

"What, and you have no one?" Anger darkened Ty's voice.

"That isn't what I meant, and you know it."

Ty held onto his temper by a thin thread. Since finding his mate, his emotions were more on edge, especially when it came to her. The large living room that only a few days earlier held over two dozen of their soldiers closed in around Raja.

"We don't have time for this now. Tabitha, get rid of the thought. It isn't happening. I'll lock you in one of the cells until this is over if you even think about leaving the grounds. I'll do whatever I can to save Bethany, but you're our first concern." Raja glanced at his Alphas briefly and then turned his attention to the laptop screen where the girl's face still stared up at him. He'd find a way to keep both Tabitha safe as well as rescue the girl before it was too late.

Bethany. I love the way it rolls off the tongue. I wonder if she's as sweet as the name. Raja shook his head to clear the thoughts. He didn't have time to think about what she might taste like. "Felix, go to my room, there's a black box on the dresser. Bring it here. Then find out where Connor stands on locating the transmission." Raja realized he still held his handgun. His pajama pants didn't have the elastic to keep the gun at the small of his back as he would prefer. "And grab my gun harness. It should be on the dresser as well."

"Now you, Tabitha, sit down. We need to discuss a few things. I need some coffee to think straight." He didn't bother to ask for some. This was his home away from home. He made his way to the kitchen, with the weight of the world on his shoulders. Pulling the coffee beans out of the freezer, he measured out enough to make a full pot. "I know we've told you that all tiger shifters will cease to exist if you're killed before you can carry on your line. So why would you be willing to risk everyone's life?"

"I can't let someone die in my place." Her compassion was commendable. He understood her desire to save the girl, he shared it, but they couldn't allow her to risk her life to save another.

"Then to save one person you would sacrifice hundreds, if not more, tiger shifters? You have to admit that doesn't make a lot of sense." Raja hit the start button on the coffee machine. As the smell of coffee filled the air, he considered their options.

"You should be able to understand this. You put your life on the line every day to protect the clan members." Tabitha begged him with her eyes, begged him to understand risking everything.

"No, Tabitha." Ty ended the argument and pulled her into his arms. She lost the fight against her wild emotions and tears flowed freely down her face. Mated couples could calm each other through touch. "You will stay here. Raja will do what he can. But we have to protect everyone."

"My Queen, you're a strong and brave woman, but you are our Queen. It's our—*my* duty to protect you. We'll do our best to save this girl and to stop whoever Pierce has behind this abduction, but for us to be able to focus on that we need to know you are safe." Raja knew it was a cold comfort he offered, but it was all he had.

The coffee machine had a pause button. He hit it and filled up three mugs before letting it finish its duty. He passed mugs to Tabitha and Ty before claiming his own. The first sip hit his tongue, making him want to purr with appreciation. Strong, dark coffee was a gift from Heaven.

"I'm not going to do anything stupid," Tabitha stated in a reluctant tone, folding her hands around her own mug.

Just in time. Felix entered, handing over the stuff to Raja.

"Good. Then you won't have a problem wearing this," Raja said, slipping the lid off the black box before passing it to Tabitha.

Inside the box laid a plain silver bracelet on black tissue paper. Ty eyed him suspiciously.

"A bracelet?" The questioning tone sounded in Tabitha's voice.

"Yes. It has a tracer installed in it. That way we'll always know where you are. I want it to never leave your wrist."

"How does it work?"

"I created an app for my cell phone, and once the tracer is activated, you will show up as a little dot." He pulled his cell phone out of his pocket, hitting a few buttons before handing it to Tabitha. "Tora has one. That's her dot. Yours would be a different color. We can also install it on Ty's and Felix's phones."

Leaning against the kitchen counter, he watched Tabitha mull the idea over. He knew she was trying to come up with a reason not to wear it, but he wasn't going to let her off the hook unless Ty decided to back his mate.

"I think this is a good idea." Ty poured himself a second cup of coffee.

"You would like to see me on a leash." It wasn't a question but a statement. "How did Tora ever agree to this?"

"Marcus and I didn't leave her a lot of choice." He frowned remembering the events that led up to the tracker bracelet for Tora. "Before we moved to Alaska, some of Pierce's clan attacked. We couldn't find Tora and thought they got her. Marcus was almost insane with anger. Turns out your mate is pretty good in battle." Raja chuckled. "He got her out of danger. Nearly died protecting her. I can never repay Ty for saving her that night."

"It was nothing. You would have done the same if it was the other way around." Ty's hand went to the scar that marred his chest from that attack. "Tabby, this will help us keep you safe."

"So what do you say? You going to wear it?" Raja pushed the box closer to her.

"I don't think I have a choice. Ty seems convinced this is needed." Reaching in the box, she pulled out the bracelet and put it on her wrist. "Happy?"

Raja leaned over the counter to her wrist. He pulled out a little pin from the bracelet that she didn't notice. "Now I'm happy." Her little dot showed up on the screen of Raja's phone.

"I'll get my phone, and you can put that app on there." Ty strolled toward the bedroom.

"Great, now I'll never get rid of him," she teased.

Raja let out a heartfelt laugh. "It's a good thing you don't want to get rid of him."

They finished programming Ty's phone when Connor and Felix rushed in. "We got the location," Connor slid to a halt in front of them.

Raja's heart skipped a beat with thoughts of what if it was too late. The pain in Bethany's eyes was enough to break his heart. He'd seen a lot of suffering and tragic events, but the video of the girl cut deep into his soul.

"Where are they?" Raja's voice sliced through the air like a dagger.

"On the other side of Fairbanks. It seems to be a remote hunting cabin."

"I'll suit up and leave immediately." Raja was all ready heading for the door.

"You?" Ty asked.

"Yes. I'll scope out the location. See if they're still there. If not, I'll track their scent."

"We can send a team to do that. There's no reason you have to be the one."

"It's something I have to do." Raja didn't know how to explain it, but he had to do this. He needed to be the one to find the girl and to make sure the man who'd hurt her paid with his life.

Tabitha laid a hand on her mate's arm. "Ty let him go. Raja, don't do anything to get yourself killed. We can send in a team. We need you."

He nodded to them before jogging out the door. He had to get to his room, suit up and be gone before Ty changed his mind.

Chapter Six

"You want to run, do you?" Her captor held her in place by her hair and screamed in her ear. Tears streamed down her face, anxiety clogged her throat and made it hard to breathe.

"Please…" Her plea died when he sat on her chest and wrapped his free hand around her throat.

"Begging for your life, are you? It will do you no good. I only need you for a few more hours and then your life will be worthless."

"This will ensure you don't try to run." He wielded a steel bar.

God help me. He's going to kill me. Mom, I should have listened to you. If I get out of this, I'll never doubt you again.

He placed the steel bar to her neck. "I could push this against your throat until you couldn't breathe. Your death would bring you peace. That's what you want, isn't it?"

"I don't want to die." She whispered, terrified of aggravating him further.

"You'll be begging for death before long." He raised the bar from her neck. Rising, he raised the bar above his head.

Every instinct screamed at her to get out of the way before he used the bar to beat her head in. Fear froze her veins and she couldn't. He slammed the steel bar down on her knee. A ragged scream ripped from her throat. Blinding hot pain pulsed from her knee, and nausea rolled her stomach.

He slapped her hard across the face with his free hand. "Don't think I'm going to let you pass out. That would be getting off easy. I enjoy the sweet smell of your pain." He leaned close, breathing in her scent. "We have so many other things we can do," the lust apparent in his voice.

Not for the first time since waking up in the strange cabin did she wonder what she was doing here. She didn't know him, and when she asked what he wanted he terrified her, because all he wanted was 'your screams.'

* * *

Raja settled into position in time to see Bethany's captor slam a pipe into her knee. He swallowed a roar or risked alerting them to his presence. A surprise attack would be the only way to get Bethany out alive.

No time to wait for back up. He sent a fast text message to Ty.

One man with her. I'm going in. Life or death.

He scoped out the area, preparing his plan. The girl wouldn't be able to walk, which meant he'd have to carry her. If others arrived, he wouldn't be able to defend them and carry her. *So I'll have to make sure he's dead and can't call backup.*

Fighting on two legs required a different style. He holstered his gun, preferring to use a knife when it came to hand-to-hand combat.

Bethany, I'm coming for you. Creeping up to the side of the cabin, he leaned back, lifted his leg and kicked the door in.

"What the fuck?"

"Get away from her." He roared. When he didn't move, Raja launched at the other man, and drove him away from Bethany. Tumbling with the man across the room, Raja slammed him into the back wall and bounced the man's head off the logs. "I warned you."

A citrus scent filled the room. The wildly out of place odor attracted him, punching through his concentration. Shaking it off, Raja focused on his prisoner.

"What do you want?" Blood gushing from his head wound, the captor sagged against the wall.

"Your life. But first tell me who hired you."

"Hired me?" The captor played stupid as if Raja couldn't smell the lie on him.

"Tell me who hired you and I'll kill you quickly. Play games with me and I'll draw it out for hours, maybe days. Now who hired you?" Raja banged the man against the wall again, hoping to make his point clear.

"It was a friend of a friend who needed me to keep the girl here until they got something they were after."

"Name?" Raja barely held his fraying temper in check. Bethany's presence was all that kept him from ripping the man's limbs off. He could smell that she was barely hanging on to consciousness behind him.

"The friend said it was for a man named Pierce, but I never met him." His voice cracked with fear. "Please, man, I wasn't going to hurt her."

"You already hurt her!" Raja snapped his neck.

* * *

She watched the scene play out before her as if watching a movie. None of it seemed real until her captor slid to the floor with a heavy plop, his neck at an odd angle. She wanted to scream, to beg for her life, but all she could do was hope it would end quickly.

"Bethany."

The man with long black hair called to her as she tried to scoot away. The pain became unbearable, making moving impossible as blackness started to fill her vision.

"Please…" She inched across the floor, every motion sparking a fresh wave of pain.

"I'm not here to hurt you."

Twisting, she fought to escape, but her knee collided with the floor and blackness swallowed her prayers to live.

Chapter Seven

Raja looked down at Bethany's still form with the same longing Ty spoke of after finding Tabitha. The citrus smell was stronger the closer he got to her. *She can't be…my mate.*

He needed to get her to a safe location. Grabbing a blanket off the nearby couch, he wrapped it around her. Her badly injured knee left him no way to carry her gently. *Good thing she's unconscious.*

He grabbed his cell and sent Ty another message so a team didn't show up after he left.

Girl's badly injured but alive. Back soon. Have Doc ready.

Message sent, he lifted her into his arms. It was a short trek to his SUV on the other side of the mountain…short for him, but brutal for her. The sooner he got her back to the compound and seen by the doctor, the more chance they might be able to save her knee.

What a time to find my mate. Life was dangerous for the Alaskan Tigers, and adding a human to the mix with no training to protect herself seemed wrong. Hot on the hells of that thought came a swift possessiveness, he wouldn't—couldn't let her go. Even in her unconscious state, her pain was palpable and ground into him. He would have given anything to end the pain.

A moan escaped her lips, and he sped up, hoping to make it to the SUV before she woke. No such luck. She cried out. Her fear of *him* slammed into him like a tsunami on a beach.

"Shhh, Bethany. I promise I'm not going to hurt you. I'm trying to get you help. We're almost there. Bear with me a little bit longer."

"Who are you? How did you know he kidnapped me?" The words rode hard breaths of air, and he almost wished she wouldn't talk. It hurt her more.

"I'm Raja. He sent the video message to us."

"Us?"

"It's a long story. Don't worry about it right now. Focus on your breathing. I can see the SUV. Almost there. I have a doctor waiting on standby."

"You're taking me to a hospital?"

"Something like that."

"Please, I want to go home," she moaned.

"We'll deal with that, but first we need to take care of you."

The sun was high on the horizon by the time he eased her into the back seat. He grabbed the bag with supplies. "This is going to hurt, but you need to keep your knee elevated." He slipped the bag under her leg, and then reached across and finagled the seat belt, doing his best to lock her in place. Once she was secure, he headed to the driver's side.

* * *

At the compound, Doctor Jacobs waited in his medical suite in the main building along with Tabitha, Ty, and Felix. Raja carried Bethany in and laid her on the bed.

"What the hell happened to her?" Doctor Jacobs demanded.

Her left eye was starting to swell shut, her lip was broken and bruised, abrasions and cuts covered her body and her knee—God her knee was a mess.

Raja growled, and Jacobs took a step back. Everyone stared at him.

"Shit! She's your mate," Ty figured out the issue first. "I can smell it all over you."

Raja didn't say anything. No point in denying it, but he wasn't ready to admit it. He was having a hard time coming to terms with it himself.

"Out." Doc ordered.

"What?" Hostility surged through Raja.

"You heard me. If you're her mate, I want you out of here."

"Being her mate gives me more reason to stay." Raja growled. He refused to abandon her—helpless and alone.

"Raja, he's right. Being her mate will only make this harder for you. We can't delay treatment. I'll stay with her and when she wakes up, I'll make sure you're here." Tabitha soothed, sidestepping closer to he and Bethany.

"There's no choice in the matter. I'm ordering you out. You won't risk this girl for your stubbornness. I would hope you would do the same for me if Tabitha was lying in that bed." Sympathy thickened Ty's voice.

"I'll be right outside and I want to know the minute she wakes up." Raja stalked out the door, his heart breaking with each step.

Chapter Eight

"Raja." Tabitha woke him with a gentle touch along his arm.

He woke, needing a moment to orient himself. He was on a couch in the clinic area. "Bethany?"

"Bethany's out of surgery and resting comfortably. I thought you might want to be with her when she wakes up."

He shot up, desperate to be with her. Being apart tore at his insides.

"Raja," Tabitha said, laying a hand on his arm. "Don't overexcite her. Give her time to recover before you scare her with the mate thing. She's been through a lot."

She was right, but it would be damn hard to keep it from her. Mates thrived under each other's touch. Bethany had no way of understanding and he wouldn't be able to stop himself from touching her for long. Hell, he knew what to expect and it terrified and thrilled him in the same breath.

"One last thing. Doc says if you stress her out, you'll be removed. She just had surgery and needs to rest. Don't make it any harder on her."

The order irked him. "I can handle my own mate." He ran his hand through his hair. "I'm sorry, Tabitha. I'm not used to this possessive attitude."

"Adjusting to the mating is the hardest part, but it will happen. Go be with your mate. I'll be back later to check on her. Being surrounded by big burly men can intimidate a girl. I'm sure a friendly woman's face will help."

"Thank you." He smiled at her before hurrying to the private rooms.

Bethany's still form looked so small and fragile in the large bed. Her face was as white as the blanket covering her. He sat in the chair next to the bed, wrapped her hand in his and lowered his head.

My mate. He loved how that flowed through his mind. *Will she accept me once she finds out what I am? Can I claim my rightful spot with her when I know the danger that will put her in? If not, am I strong enough to walk away from her?*

The questions circling in his mind plagued him. He knew the answers to two out of three. He wasn't strong enough to walk away from her, no matter the danger it would put her in. He would protect her with his life. Could he convince Bethany that she was meant for him and they belonged together? That was another story entirely.

It hit him like a bear at full speed what Ty must be going through with Tabitha. The constant fear that he could be the reason that his mate was in danger weighed heavily in the pit of his stomach.

"Bethany, believe in me and I'll make you the happiest woman alive. I'll protect you with my life. Don't turn away from me when you find out what I really am." Raja whispered. Bringing her knuckles to his lips, he placed a timid kiss there.

* * *

Raja paced the small room, feeling like a caged tiger. The walls growing closer with each passing hour that Bethany lay unconscious. The nurse assured him it was the drugs from the surgery and nothing to worry about. That did nothing to calm the raging tiger inside of him. His mate was injured and he could do nothing, but sit by and wait.

Waiting wasn't something he handled well. He needed action.

A soft moan came from the bed. In two quick strides, Raja advanced to the bedside, her hand in his. "Bethany, you're safe. Come on, open your eyes." He looked but she didn't seem to have moved. *Now I'm hearing things because I want it to happen.*

Moaning again, her eyelids fluttered as if she were desperate to see her surroundings.

"Come on, sweetie. That's it."

"Where am I?" Her voice roughened. She struggled to take in her surroundings.

The room was more like a bedroom than a hospital. Shifters healed fast, so medical attention was only required at a minimal level.

When they crafted the building, they wanted it to feel like home, not a hospital. They didn't have a large medical staff, only what they needed, including Doc, and could take care of anything including performing surgeries.

"You're somewhere safe. That's what matters."

"This isn't a hospital." Her eyes held terror again. Her hair spread over the pillow, and he wanted to lean in close for a better smell of the citrus encircling her.

"Bethany, trust me. You're safe. You had surgery and shouldn't overdo it. Rest. I promise I'll be here by your side when you wake up. Nothing will happen to you."

"You expect me to rest? How do I know you're not teamed with the guy who took me hostage? Maybe you wanted me all to yourself, that's why..." Her voice trailed off.

"I killed him? That's ludicrous. I saved your life, and brought you here, Doc performed surgery on your knee, and you'll walk again. Why would I risk my ass to save you, only to kill you myself? Why would we waste the time and effort for the surgery if we were going to kill you? If that's what we were going to do then why not leave you to suffer?"

She seemed flabbergasted by the questions.

"I want to help you. I swear you are someplace safe."

"I asked you to take me to a hospital."

"Did you not hear him say he was hired by someone? That someone would know you escaped and would be looking for you? It wouldn't take long to find you lying in a hospital bed with a busted knee. You would be helpless there, drugged, unable to escape. Is that how you want to die?" Raja knew he was being harsh, but if she didn't see the truth soon she could cause problems. If she tried to leave, she could get herself killed, and he would be damned if he was going to let that happen.

"I don't want to die." Lonely fear etched into every word.

"Let me protect you, at least until you are back on your feet. You have to know you're helpless in the condition you're in." *Until you're back on your feet, my ass. It will give me enough time to convince you that you're mine. Then you won't want to be anywhere, but in my arms.*

She watched him, her terror giving way to something inscrutable. He couldn't tell if she was angry that he wanted to protect her—or that she was helpless in the first place. Maybe both.

"Bethany, you need help. Let me help you." He reached for her hand, and she didn't pull away.

She nodded, still fighting to keep her eyes open.

"Rest. I'll be here keeping you safe. I won't leave your side." He rubbed his thumb over the back of her hand in small circles.

A sizzle of electricity passed from his hand into hers, making her eyes fly open.

"What was that?"

"Sorry, I think I shocked you." *Finally a sign that she's truly my mate.*

"It felt like I put my hand in the electric socket." Her voice dulled, heavy with sleep and her eyes closed again.

"It just startled you because you were so close to sleep." The jolt of electricity was what he needed. *She's mine.*

Chapter Nine

"How is she doing?" Tabitha asked from the doorway. Her mate stood behind her, his hand resting gently on her hip. Mates liked physical contact with each other.

"Better. At least I think I convinced her I'm not going to kill her." It had been too long since his last restful night's sleep, and it had taken a toll on Raja.

"I can sit with her a while if you want to lie down." Tabitha stepped into the room.

"Thank you, but I'd rather just sleep in the chair. I promised her I wouldn't leave and lying to your mate probably isn't a good way to start." He tried to smile, making light of the whole thing but Tabitha didn't buy it.

"I understand, but you won't be any good to her or us if you are worn out. You know where I am if you change your mind, send me a text and I'll be down in minutes."

His Queen was right but leaving his mate when she needed him the most felt like betrayal.

"Ty, if I could stay with her until she's awake, I'll get another guard to watch over her so I can deal with my duties."

Ty held up his hand. "It's fine. Your mate needs you. If things change with the Pierce situation, then you might need another guard to watch her. But for now stay with your mate, and get some rest. I need you at your best if there's an attack."

"Thank you, sir." His Alpha's concern and understanding touched him.

"The sister is arriving tomorrow afternoon. I'll want you in on that meeting. Tabitha and her guards can watch over Bethany. I'm sure some female bonding time will be good for her."

Raja nodded. He had to be at that meeting. Pierce's sister might provide information they needed. He couldn't let finding his mate jeopardize the clan. After what happened to Bethany and the attacks on Tabitha, taking Pierce down was imperative.

"I brought you this because I know sitting around waiting for someone to wake up isn't the best. I thought you might want to be able to work. It might help keep your mind off things and bring us one step closer to Pierce." Tabitha handed him a bag that he hadn't realized she held.

"Thank you. I appreciate it. I was starting to climb the walls." He placed the bag on the bedside table, knowing he would find his laptop and notes in it. Tabitha was always well attuned with the needs and desires of others.

"Lukas's brother sent another transmission. You should find it in your email. Unfortunately this one wasn't in time to stop the attack…it was about Bethany."

A growl escaped before he could get ahold of it. "Did he mention her by name?"

Ty shook his head. "But it implies she'll only be the first of many."

"With a little luck, having to find another to do his dirty work will slow him down. The guy who kidnapped Bethany is dead so he won't be doing anyone's dirty work any longer."

* * *

It was after eleven o'clock at night when Bethany woke and found Raja asleep on the chair next to the bed. His neck canted at an uncomfortable angle, his hand still wrapped around hers, and a laptop on his lap.

He didn't leave. If he wanted to harm me, would he really be sitting here passed out in the chair, holding my hand? Something was different about him. Earlier, his face held such concern for her. *Why would he care about me?* But despite his concern, she also knew that he hadn't been entirely straightforward with her.

She caught a glimpse of her cell on the nightstand. *If I can only reach it without waking him, I can call home.* Angling slightly, careful not to jar the bed, she reached for the phone.

Her fingers closed around the phone when a throat cleared behind her. She almost dropped it in her haste to move away.

"Planning to call someone?" Raja sat there in the chair watching her as if she was under a microscope.

"Umm…"

"You're not a prisoner here, Bethany. You can call someone without sneaking around."

"Well then…" She unlocked the phone and pulled up her contact list.

"How about you wait until morning? If you're calling your family, it's past four in the morning there."

Her hands dropped in defeat.

"What are you going to tell them anyway?"

"Umm…" She hadn't thought of that. *Shit I haven't thought that far. What am I going to tell them?*

"Wow, you have it all planned out. Don't you?"

"I'm going to ask my father to come get me. He can fly out here and help me get back home." She was proud she was able to come up with something so quickly. But she wasn't sure if it was the truth. Would she have been able to tell her mom, her bad feelings were right and now she needed to be saved? She would hear about that until the end of time.

"Are you going to tell them you were kidnapped? How your knee got busted?"

"What do you care what I tell my parents?" Frustration filled her. *Damn it, I just want to go home.*

"I care because I killed the man who did this to you, remember?"

"If you're worried I'm going to turn you in, don't. You helped me when I couldn't have done it myself. I'm trying to rid you of the problem. I'll tell them it was a snowboarding accident."

"I'm not worried about myself. I'm worried about you. You leave here and you'll have a bull's eye on your back."

"I don't see how it matters if I'm here or back with my family. This asshole will still want me. At least back home I have the upper hand. I know the lay of the land and have people who will protect me." She leaned back against the pillow.

"No one can protect you like I can. Plus we're already on the trail to finding this bastard."

"Oh a He-man who thinks he's the only one good enough for the job." She let out a puff of air, blowing the hair away from her face.

"I don't think. I know." He growled at her.

She sank back into the bed, wishing it would swallow her whole. Anything to get away from him.

"I'm sorry. It's just that I don't want to see you hurt worse or possibly killed."

"Oh and you think I do?"

"You're sure as hell acting like you don't value your life very much." He set the laptop on the stand and stood. "If you would just trust me, we'll deal with the situation while you're recovering, and then you can do what you want."

She met him at the worst possible point of her life, how was she supposed to trust him when her whole sense of trust was just thrown out the window. "Who is we?"

"There is a group of us that live here together. I don't know how you got dragged into this, but the man behind your kidnapping it someone we have been hunting for a while. He's very dangerous and has killed before. Taking your life…he wouldn't lose a night's sleep over it."

"What did you do to him?"

"It wasn't what we did to him. It was more like what he did to us. It's a long story."

Anger twined with pain in his voice. *What happened to him to have such pain in his voice?* "Tell me."

"Another time." He reached up and tied his hair back with a leather strap. "How are you feeling? Are you in pain?" Deflecting the topic, she understood and for now she let it slide. She didn't have the strength to fight him now.

"Not real pain. I feel drunk more than anything."

"It's the pain medication. It will make you think you can fly if you let it." He smiled down at her for the first time.

Wow, what an amazing smile. It could light up the darkest room. "You have a beautiful smile. You should use it more often."

"You're starting to sound like Tora."

I can't believe my luck—he's married. She glanced at his left hand, but saw no wedding band. *Not every man wears his ring. I should know that better than anyone.*

As if he caught her looking at his hand, he smiled again. "Tora's my sister."

"Your sister?" She couldn't keep the surprise out of her voice.

"Yes. She's married to Marcus, and they have a beautiful daughter, Scarlet."

Happiness and love filled his voice. His whole being seemed to come alive when he spoke of them. "You seem close to them. How old is Scarlet?"

"I am. Tora and I have been through a lot together over the years and Scarlet's fourteen months, and she has her Uncle Raja wrapped tightly around her little finger."

It wasn't hard to imagine him as the doting uncle. She loved children and hoped someday to have some of her own. "In your tone I can hear how much you adore Scarlet. Any children of your own?"

"Not yet." He laughed. "Someday, I want a few dozen of my own."

"Dozen?" Shock rippled through her at the multiplication of her thought.

"Yeah, why not?"

She let out a heartfelt laugh. "You better find a few very understanding women to give you that many. I doubt one woman would want to go through a dozen pregnancies."

"I guess when I find the right woman, I'll take as many munchkins as she will give me."

Uncomfortable, she tried to readjust, and pain shot through her.

Raja closed his hand over hers and the pain subsided.

"What just happened?" A fresh wave of surprise pulsed through her.

"You're not due for another pain pill for any hour, but if you're in that much pain I'll get Doc. Surely there's something he could do for you."

"Raja, you ignored my question. You know what I'm talking about. Answer me."

"It's nothing." He sat back into the chair he recently vacated.

"Don't tell me it's nothing. It's something and you don't want to tell me." She wanted him to touch her again, to make the pain disappear. She didn't know how it worked, but it felt wonderful to be pain free.

Chapter Ten

How am I supposed to tell a human that knows nothing about shifters that I'm her mate and I can help take away her pain? This is insane. It's dangerous and could expose us all. This isn't just risking my ass but everyone's. Tabitha is in enough danger, she doesn't need more. Raja rose and paced around the small room, as he played out the outcomes to the problem in his mind.

"What is your problem, why won't you be straight with me?" Irritation laced Bethany's voice mirroring the agitation he could feel building within.

"Bethany…" Raja growled and stopped, reining in his temper. "You don't understand what you're asking. This involves more than just me."

"If you're not going to be straight with me, I'd like you to leave."

"Everyone wants something, but babe, you don't have a chance in hell of getting that. So get some rest and we'll deal with the rest of this crap tomorrow." Raja stopped at the foot of the bed, glaring down at her.

"I don't want to sleep." But her body betrayed her. Here eyelids drooped and she tried, but failed to stifle a yawn.

"It's the best thing for you. The faster you will heal, the quicker you'll get back on your feet." Her eyes closed heavily. "Sleep, my sweet Bethany," he whispered as she drifted to sleep.

I wanted a mate with spirit. He just hadn't expected her to be fragile or broken or so determined to assert her own authority when he met her. *A full human to boot. How am I supposed to handle this?*

The hair on the back of Raja's neck stood up. Glancing behind him at the doorway, he found Shadow standing just beyond the frame. Shadow may have barely turned twenty, but her life was hard before she came to their clan. She spent much of it on the street, working odd jobs to keep food in her stomach. Yet, she still possessed a childlike innocence to her. She tried to find the good in everyone, but get on her bad side and watch out. She could be as vicious as any male shifter in a heartbeat.

"Shadow, what are you doing here so late?"

"Doc asked me to look in on the patient. He mentioned she was human and wanted to make sure there wasn't anything going on inside her that his test wouldn't show." In her oversized University of Alaska sweatshirt and leggings, she looked more like a college student than one of their best guards.

Doc didn't mean medical. Shadow wouldn't have been useful in a medical emergency. Her abilities lay in the psyche. She was still relatively new to the Alaskan Tiger's Clan, and Raja hadn't had the time to get to know her that well, but she already made a name for herself.

"Is that implying the rumors I heard are true?"

"I'm don't know what rumors you've heard, sir. But I'm sure not all of them are true." Reserved, Shadow spoke in a low tone. At least she spoke. When she first arrived, she didn't.

"I've heard you can tell everything about a person from looking into their soul—everything from their past, future, and even their destined mate. True?"

"To a degree. I know their conscious and unconscious minds. If I have met both of them, then yes I know who their mate is, even before the mating ritual takes place. I cannot say I know everything about a person. People are surprising creatures." She stepped into the room, nearing the bed. She closed her eyes, and her long dark hair fell forward, blocking her face from Raja's view.

"Doc has nothing to worry about. She is and will be fine." She walked to the doorway and paused. "Sir, may I speak freely?"

Raja nodded. If she didn't feel it was important enough to risk the wrath of an Elder, she wouldn't have asked.

"Be up front with her. She can handle it. Subconsciously she already knows of shifters." With that, she left, Raja alone with his thoughts.

Could she handle the truth?

Marissa Dobson

Chapter Eleven

Bethany woke to find a strange woman sitting by her bedside, and Raja nowhere in sight. *Great, he decided to take my advice and leave. Why send this woman...unless I'm a prisoner here.*

"Morning, Bethany."

Wow, someone is excessively chipper in the morning. She glanced at the bedside clock. "Two in the afternoon." It was too late to call her parents. They would have already left for the weekend trip to their mountain cabin and out of touch for the next few days.

"Raja left me with detailed instructions. I wasn't supposed to wake you. He said you needed your rest after a rough night."

"He'll be back? Who are you?"

"I'm Tabitha. Yes, he should be back shortly. He's meeting with my sweetie and some of the...um...employees."

"I don't mean to sound rude, but why are you here?" Was Raja telling her the truth when he said she wasn't a prisoner here?

"He asked me to sit with you in case you needed something. Doc says you can't put any weight on that knee for at least forty-eight hours. With you stuck in bed, having someone here with you seemed like a good idea. Plus after being stuck with Raja all this time, I thought you could use some girl bonding." Tabitha let out a laugh.

Bethany might not be a prisoner, but she couldn't get up and leave either. She lay back against the pillow with a sigh.

"If you prefer I left..."

"No, you're fine. I hate being stuck in this bed."

Tabitha nodded. "I bet you could talk Raja into taking you out of this room for a while when he gets back."

Bethany gave her a smile. Tabitha meant well, but Raja...well, she didn't want to deal with him if he couldn't be straight with her. If she was supposed to trust a stranger, he needed to be honest with her. "I doubt that. Raja and I don't see eye to eye."

"He can be stubborn, but he's a good man and has his reason for his actions. Anything I can do to help you deal with him?" Tabitha leaned forward to pour a glass of water from the bedside pitcher.

"I doubt that." She thought about the night before as Tabitha poured them each a drink. "I'm not in some voodoo colony or something, am I?"

The woman let out a wholehearted laugh. "I'm sorry. What gives you that idea?"

"Something that happened last night. It was weird."

"You mean the pain leaving with his touch?" She handed her the cup of water.

"How did you know about that?" Bethany eyed Tabitha.

"Raja was still grumbling about it when I came down here."

"What caused it? It was the weirdest sensation."

"Bethany, honestly I would like to tell you. To explain everything to you and be able to answer all your questions..."

"But you won't," Bethany interrupted.

"Correct. I won't. Raja will be back soon, and I promise he'll tell you the truth. It's something you should hear from him. However, I can tell you this. Something similar happened to me, but I wouldn't change the outcome for the world. Trust in Raja, and you won't be disappointed."

Doubtful, Bethany tired of the run-around. *Maybe when Raja comes back I won't want to hear the answer to my questions. Who am I trying to kid? I want to know.*

* * *

Two floors above, Raja fought to keep his temper from blowing. Pierce's sister, Jessica, worked his last nerve. "Your brother killed people, do you realize that? He'll keep killing unless you help us." He slammed his hand on the table, making the papers jump.

"He's still my baby brother. I don't want to see him killed because of what your kind did to him." Jessica sat there in near tears, playing with the bottom button on her jacket.

"Miss Black," Ty sat across the table. "Your brother isn't killing out of revenge. He's killing because he knows no other way. He was never taught the way to handle the beast inside of him. In time, the beast took over. The man he is now is not your brother. He's suffering; the beast is making him insane. He's rabid."

"He's still my brother." She argued.

"I wish I could agree with you. I wish I could tell you there was hope for him. But you have to know deep in your soul that there's nothing you can do for him. With your education and training, you have to realize he's lost." Ty leaned forward in his chair, meeting her gaze.

"I won't give up on him."

Ty continued to hold her gaze, as he spoke. "Miss Black, if there was anything I could do to help you save your brother…if you would have come to me sooner I would have done it, but that time has passed. It isn't too late to protect the innocents."

"You people are not innocent. Look at what your kind did to Pierce." She yelled, tears sliding down her cheeks.

"The shifter who attacked your brother was rabid. Like your brother, he let the beast take control. Once we were aware of the situation, the subject was terminated. The former leader tried to help your brother, and in return for his efforts, he and his wife were killed. Leaving an innocent child an orphan."

Those deaths were news to her. Shock blazed in her eyes like lanterns on a dark night and she clapped a hand over her mouth. Pierce likely only told her things to make her feel sorry for him, not anything that might turn her against him.

"I need some time." She relented.

"We'll have a guard show you to your room. All we ask is that you don't contact Pierce. We have innocent women and children here."

She nodded and stood.

"Miss Black," Raja called as she neared the door, "don't wait too long. Pierce will attack again, and I'd hate for another innocent woman to be caught in his wrath. The next one might not be as lucky as Bethany."

Chapter Twelve

"She slept the whole time?" Raja headed straight for Bethany as soon as the meeting ended and Ty followed in his wake.

"No, she was up for a bit. She is impatient about what happened last night. Tell her, Raja." Tabitha's face softened with love and she rose, almost flowing into her mate's embrace. Before he met Bethany, Raja hadn't realized how much he envied Ty that connection.

"I will, but I'm not waking her up to tell her."

"It doesn't look like you have to, she's waking." Ty clasped Raja's shoulder, a show of support before ushering his mate out.

"Cowards!" Raja called to them earning a matching pair of smug smiles before they closed the door.

"Tabitha left?" Sleep laced Bethany's voice.

"Yeah. You're stuck with me now." He handed her a glass of water.

She took a long drink, watching him over the rim. "It could be worse." She handed him the now empty glass in return.

"I don't believe that was your sentiment last night."

"Speaking of last night…"

"Wait a moment, Bethany. We can discuss that, but first I need you to understand that what I'm about to tell you will come as a shock. There's no easy way to tell you, and I'm taking an enormous risk by doing so. Hundreds will be in jeopardy if this gets out. Worse, we would become prey and likely exterminated if the government learned of our existence."

"Raja, you make this sound like you're some escaped lab experiment or something. You helped me, and whatever it is, your secret is safe with me. Please tell me what the hell is going on."

He wanted to believe her. He needed to believe. Revealing their secrets went against every ounce of his training, but he couldn't live with lying to his mate—even his mate potential. Trusting Shadow and Tabitha, he sucked in a deep breath. "I'm a shapeshifter, a tiger to be exact."

She raised an eyebrow, clearly suspicious. "Is that like a were-wolf?"

"Were-animals can only change according to the moon. Shifters can change at will."

"Prove it." Challenging him, she was beautiful and formidable even with her injuries.

"Now?" Raja asked, confused that she wasn't demanding he take her to the nearest airport. *Shouldn't she be freaked out about this or something?*

"Yes, now. You said the moon doesn't control you. If it's true, then do it. Or are you a few marbles short? Maybe you need to be placed in a padded cell?"

"I'm not mental." He growled at her. For the first time in days, he let his inner tiger spring free. He usually saved his shifts for his evening runs, allowing the tiger the freedom they both wanted. Letting the tiger out invigorated his soul.

His body shifted and reshaped into the tiger form. Relief banished his discomfort and anxiety. On four legs he experienced only freedom as though his human form were a too tight pair of shoes. Shaking out his coat, and tossing what was left of his shredded clothes off, he padded over to Bethany, nudging her hand with his nose.

He studied her reaction, expecting to see horror and found only wonder. Her eyes lit up with excitement, instead of the panic he had imagined.

"No way!" Bethany touched the top of his head and ran her fingers through his fur. "I always thought Dad was off his rocker. He said things like this existed, but I never believed him. He told me one day I would find out for myself." Laughing, she used her nails to massage his head, scratching right up and around his ears. "Guess he was right. Can you understand me when you're like that?"

He purred, delighted and relieved at her response.

Raja wasn't sure how long they stayed like that. He was perfectly content in his tiger form, with her rubbing his head. He felt almost like a big housecat as he leaned against the bed and let her pet him while she chatted on about her father's stories. Shadow's scent drifted up the hallway and he turned to face the door, ready to defend his mate.

"What is it?" Bethany's hand stopped in Raja's thick fur.

Shadow appeared in the doorway.

"I brought you a pair of scrubs. It's all we have down here. There's an emergency meeting in the conference room in ten minutes. Tabitha and her guards are on their way." She set the scrubs on the chair before hurrying away.

Raja shifted, his back to Bethany. Slipping on the scrub pants before turning to face her. He eyed the shirt, knowing it wouldn't fit, and left it on the chair. "I'm sorry. I'm sure you have a ton of questions. I promise I'll answer them when I get back."

She nodded. "What's going on?"

"I don't know, but it is nothing for you to worry about. You're safe here."

"Tabitha, is she…"

"I don't have enough time to explain that one. Ask her." The worried look in her eyes tugged at him. "Bethany, you're safe here."

"But am I safe without you?"

"You're worried the others here will attack you?"

"No. I'm wondering if anyone else would protect me like you can." She played with the edge of the blanket, not meeting his gaze.

He wanted to say that no one could protect his mate as he could, but he'd already pushed his luck. Better to let her absorb all of this in stages. The Alpha and Lieutenant's mates were guarded and protected against all threats. They were the Elders of the clan, but telling her this wouldn't ease her concerns and would only leave her with more questions.

"Tabitha is the Alpha Female. She has some of the best guards on her at all times. Nothing will happen in this room with the two of you here. I'll be back soon and when I do, there's more we need to discuss." Before he could talk himself out of it, he bent down and placed a gentle kiss on her lips. The kiss wouldn't set the meters off, but it was enough to wash her fears away. "I'll be back soon."

He reached for his weapons, strapping the knife to his thigh. He'd carry the gun because his shoulder holster lay shredded with his clothes. He'd have to grab his spare one while he was upstairs.

Tabitha entered with Adam and three other guards. Their gazes met briefly. She walked past him toward the bed, whispering a sub vocal. "There's another video."

Shit!

Chapter Thirteen

Raja found Ty, Felix, Marcus and Thomas sitting at the conference table looking shell-shocked. Connor worked on a laptop at the other end, paying no mind to anyone else. The silence hung heavily over the room, the coffee sat in front of many of them untouched. *What's in the damn video to get to these warriors? These are men I would trust my life with, and now they sit before me looking defeated.*

Sitting in the last chair, Jessica Black crunched into a ball. Her body shook violently with silent sobs as she hugged her body close to her.

"There's another video," Ty said quietly, coming to stand next to him.

He nodded. "Tabitha said. That bad?"

"Worse."

"Have Connor put a trace on it, and let's get a team there. Maybe we will get lucky again."

Ty stood there shaking his head. "Connor's tracing the place it was sent from, but we know where the video was filmed. It's too late."

"Too late?" Raja didn't want to believe it. But Ty continued to avoid making eye contact. "I need to see the video."

"It's not necessary."

"I think it is. Ty, what aren't you telling me?"

"The attack was in Virginia." Ty's gaze fell away, as if waiting for Raja's rage.

"Spit it out." Raja's nerves were on edge.

"It's Bethany's family on the video."

His heart sank. "Are they…?"

Ty nodded. "It's too late."

"I want to see the video."

Rather than sit in front of the laptop, Raja wished he could bolt to the bathroom to throw up. The fact that he was about to watch the murder of his mate's family made it that much worse. They warned him that it wasn't easy to watch. These men, whom he had been in battle with, who fought to protect the compound, were shocked. Whatever he was about to watch would haunt him.

"Was it sent to Tabitha again?"

"Jessica received it. Someone saw her with Leo and Connor."

He couldn't postpone it any longer. He slid the headphones over his ears and hit the play button.

A family room came into view, the sun shining in the windows, illuminating the photographs. Bethany at graduation in her cap and gown, standing next to people he assumed were her parents. Another of her and her sister at an amusement park. The camera scrolled through the pictures lining the mantle, pausing on each of them for a brief moment.

"Bethany's happy family, or so it would seem. Do you think anyone ever told the girls their uncle is a raving lunatic? I doubt it, but tonight everyone will know. Tonight the family will have to face the beast their uncle created." The voice over was thick with hatred, and he recognized the voice immediately as Pierce's.

The video went black, and then focused on three people sitting down at the dinner table.

"This will be the last meal they enjoy as a family. Tonight their life will end as mine did all those years ago. Poor Bethany will be begging for me to kill her when I find her."

The camera cut out again, only to come back to show the father's throat slit and the women tied to the kitchen chairs. The forgotten food scattered across the clean kitchen floor.

"The man wasn't worth my time. Tonight's about the women. They'll suffer, begging for me to kill them before they finish serving their purpose and I finish them."

He stopped narrating from behind the camera, fixing it to the table and going to the teen girl. She couldn't be older than seventeen; he pushed her long brown hair from her face giving the camera a good view of her. Fear radiated in the girls eyes as she wiggled in the chair trying to get away from him. Sniffing her neck, Pierce whispered, "How good you smell. I'm going to enjoy you."

The mother attempted a scream through her gag, begging for her daughter's life. Pierce responded by grabbing a Bowie knife off the table and throwing it at her. It found its home buried deep in her chest, below her breast.

"The fear pouring off your body smells so good. I'm going to enjoy this." Pierce's face contorted, and his fangs extended. He bit a chunk out of her neck. She violently fought against the ropes to get away, desperate to survive. He bent out of camera range. Coming up, he spit two of her fingers across the table.

He pushed the chair back enough to give a full view of the girl. He ran his hands, claws replacing fingers, across the girl's stomach. "I'm going to gut you and bathe in your blood."

Tears welled in the girl's eyes, as she looked at the camera, her gaze screaming for a mercy that would never come.

His claws broke the girl's skin. Blood gushed out, covering her legs before landing on the floor. Her eyes closed, and her breath became shallow.

"She won't get off that easy." He reached behind him, pulling out a bag with small white tubes in it. Cracking one open, he ran it under the girl's nose. "Smelling salts," he laughed.

The torture of the girl went on for what seemed like hours, but in reality lasted only minutes. Raja stared at the shocky, blanched face of his mate's sister wishing her death would come swiftly if only to spare her.

The video drew him back when Pierce's voice filled the earphones again. "I wish I had more time to play with you, Momma.

Nevertheless, you suffered enough watching your little girl die. Know this, I'll hunt Bethany down and do the same to her."

The woman looked defeated. All the fight gone from her. She had a hard time breathing, as the knife in her chest must have punctured a lung.

He sliced the woman's throat, spraying blood across the camera lens. The woman slumped in her chair as Pierce picked up the camera and tried to wipe it off.

"Dear sister of mine. You have betrayed me. Going to the ones I despise the most. Know I'll find you too. I might not make you suffer, after all, you're family, but your life will still be over. Tell me, was it worth it?"

With that, the video ended. Raja leaned back in his chair and roared.

Chapter Fourteen

Hours later the conference room was empty except for Raja and Ty. Felix had left moments before to join Tabitha with Bethany, leaving the men alone.

"Do you want Tabitha and I to stay when you tell Bethany?"

"No. I'll do it alone. Her father used to tell her stories of shifters, but I don't think she knows they were part of her family."

"If she does, she might be able to give us an idea of who he'll target next. I have the West Virginia tiger clan looking into possible relatives and connections, but it will take time."

"I'll see what I can find."

"Raja, I know what you're thinking and the answer is no." Raja stared at Ty until he continued. "You can't sit there and tell me you're not thinking of going after Pierce yourself."

"I want to be on the team that takes him down."

"No."

"What do you mean no?"

"Exactly what I said. You're too valuable to the clan. Tabitha and Bethany would never forgive me if I let something happened to you. If he attacks the compound or us then yes, you'll be expected to fight but as my Lieutenant, you aren't on the front lines any longer. Especially on this one."

Raja growled. He couldn't believe his ears.

"Growl all you want. Face it, you're mated now. Our numbers are too low to toss away a mated couple."

"Don't give me that crap."

"You wouldn't support my decision to go into the front lines either, and the whole reason he's targeting us is because my mate could be the end of the tigers."

"You are Alpha. You're not supposed to be in battle," Raja snarled, getting to his feet.

"You're my Lieutenant and valuable to the clan. Without you and Bethany, Tabitha cannot complete her mission to bring all the tigers together. Your mating was one of the steps the book mentioned that needed to be completed."

Raja was in a battle he wouldn't win, unless he wanted to fight Ty for dominance, which he did not intend to do. *There has to be a way around it without bringing Pierce to the compound.*

"Why didn't you tell me?"

"Tell you that you had to mate for things to go forward? Seriously? You would have fought the mating at every crossroads. You said you wanted nothing to do with a mate. Now, my friend, you have no choice. Your mate is downstairs waiting for you."

"I'm not sure she'll be ready to accept me after I give her the news of her family," Raja said, slid his hands into his pockets trying to calm his nerves.

* * *

"We heard a roar. What's going on?" Bethany asked, panic filling her voice.

"Tabitha, Ty's in the hall. I need to speak with Bethany alone."

"If you need anything, Raja can reach me." Tabitha stood, giving Bethany's hand a squeeze before leaving.

"What's going on?"

He closed the distance between them in three quick strides, taking her hand into his. "I told you before that we received a video, which is how we knew you were taken. Connor, our wolf computer geek, was able to trace it."

"What does that have to do with the roar I heard?"

"We received another one." Raja dropped into the chair next to the bed, his head in his hands.

"Then go save her like you did me. I'm fine. I don't need you hovering when there's another life in jeopardy."

Raja looked up, grief clogging his throat. His heart broke for her. The news he had to deliver was horrific, with no easy way to say it.

"Raja..." Concern thickened in her voice.

"It's not the same." He took a deep breath, saying a silent prayer for the strength and words to tell her.

"What do you mean?"

"Oh Bethany," he leaned in close to the bed, wrapping his hands around her small, delicate ones. Nothing would be the same for her ever again. "It's your family."

"What about them? They're home in Virginia, safe. Right?" When he didn't answer, she dug her fingers into his palm. "Tell me what's going on. You're starting to scare me."

"The man who ordered your kidnapping, Pierce—he attacked your parents' home."

"But they're fine, right?" She released him to grab for her cell on the nightstand, tears already gleaming in her eyes.

Raja recaptured her hands, not letting her reach the phone. "I'm sorry."

"No, you're wrong. They were supposed to go to the cabin…they wouldn't be home. You have to be wrong." She pleaded, tears spilling down her cheeks.

"I watched the video myself."

"Jamie? Is she okay?"

"I'm sorry."

Bethany's tears flowed freely now. Raja stood, setting his gun on the nightstand. He eased himself on the bed next to her, careful not to disturb her injured knee. He wrapped his arms around her. She snuggled into his embrace, and he held her wishing he could take this pain away as easily as the physical agony.

After a few minutes of uncontrollable tears, she turned her head away, leaving a wet spot, but he didn't mind. She tilted her head up to look at him. "I want to see the video."

"No!" he growled.

"I want to see it," she stated with more determination.

"It's out of the question. I won't let your last memories of your family be tainted by their murders. Bethany, please leave it be. I won't have it." He growled, his tiger pacing furiously inside him.

"I have a right."

"Please…" He wanted to yell at her to make her drop it, but it was the last thing she needed.

"It's that bad? You were roaring." Her voice cracked.

Raja nodded, unable to say the words.

"I'll have to go home…to deal with things."

"We'll make arrangements, but we have to wait for the police to contact you. If not they would want to know where you received your knowledge."

"Why can't we take the video to the police?"

"He shifts in it."

"To keep your secret safe, my family dies in vain? No justice for their murders?" she accused, pulling away from him.

"Your parents and sister will get justice. I'll see to that. This is bigger than you, or even your family. He killed Tabitha's parents years ago. We have been hunting him for a long time."

"He gets to run free for years? If someone would have fought for Tabitha's parents, maybe mine would be alive!" Grief and helplessness collided in her expression.

"Bethany, you know nothing of the situation," he spat at her before jerking his emotions under control. "We have been searching for him all these years. Hunting him every time a lead comes up. Until recently, we thought—hoped he was dead. We're working hard to find him and take him out of the equation."

"Why did you think he was dead?"

"He lied in wait for Tabitha. She's coming into her tiger, and he wants to stop it. That is what has brought him out of hiding."

"What does she have to do with any of it?" She shivered as if chilled.

"Come here." He rubbed her arms, hoping that she would relax in his embrace. She rested her head on his chest, tears dripping onto his chest. She belonged there. Her body fit snugly against him. "It's a long story."

"I don't have anywhere to go." She sounded so small.

Maybe the story could help distract her. Distract him. Paltry comfort that it might be. "To make a long story short, she's our Queen. If she dies before she can carry on the line, legend has it that we'll all die with her."

"She's a tiger?"

"She will be. She has the tiger in her but hasn't completed the change yet. You can feel it when you're around her that she'll shift soon." He ran his fingers up and down her arm.

"You can?"

"A shifter can. Humans wouldn't know or understand what to look for."

Chapter Fifteen

Bethany finally fell asleep in his arms, leaving him unable to get anything done. Usually sitting still left him restless, but with Bethany in his arms he experienced—contentment. He enjoyed the feeling of her body next to his.

Tabitha entered the room with the Captain of her Guards, Felix. "Ty told me what's in the video. I wanted to make sure she's all right."

"I don't think all right is the best word, but she is dealing with it the best she can. She wants to go home, to take care of things."

"I expected as much. However, Ty and I have spoken about this and don't feel it is wise at this time."

Raja's body stiffened, unable to believe what he was hearing. He didn't plan to let her travel home alone. He and a handful of guards could go with her. "You're asking her to miss her parents' and sister's funerals?"

"Not exactly. We were hoping she would agree to have the bodies flown here. Ty wants to send a team from the West Virginia clan in to search for evidence. We need to discuss this with her immediately. We also need you to find out about the uncle. See what she knows about him."

"Give me some time with her to see what I can find out, and then we can discuss her family's arrangements with her. I'm assuming you would prefer not to wait, but she's struggling here."

"Okay. You have forty minutes. I'll bring Ty back then. Unless you want to bring her upstairs. Doc agreed to allow her to move into one of the guest rooms."

"She can stay in my quarters." Raja barked.

"I guess that means you'll bring her upstairs, then?"

He nodded.

"Good. We'll see you in forty minutes in our quarters." She didn't give him time to change his mind, sweeping out with Felix in attendance.

"Love," he whispered gently, rubbing has hand against her cheek. She moaned.

"Love, I need you to wake up."

"Humm," she moaned, half asleep.

"Come on, love."

"Love?" Her eyes snapped open, but there was no anger in her voice.

"Yes, you are my love." He trailed his hand over her cheek before lowering his head toward hers and kissing her. "Now that you're awake. Do you have an uncle?"

"Dad has a brother, but I haven't seen him since I was a child. Why?"

"What's his name? Do you know where we can find him?"

"What do you want with him?" She questioned.

"Pierce mentioned him in the video. If he isn't part of this as we believe, then he's in danger."

"Uncle James was always more of a loner. I don't know where he is now, but I remember Dad saying he had a cabin in North Dakota. But what would my uncle have to do with it?"

"I'm not sure yet, but we will figure it out. I'll see if Connor can locate James. We have to meet with Ty and Tabitha upstairs. Doc said you are doing better and can move to your own room. I'd like you to stay in my quarters. You'll have your own room. I want you close so I can protect you." Raja slipped out of bed and grabbed his gun.

"Why are we meeting them?"

"To discuss your plans to travel to Virginia." He steered the wheelchair that someone had the foresight to leave in the room, close to the bed. "We'll try to get you on your feet tomorrow with crutches, but tonight you'll have to use this." He slid his arm under her legs and the other one behind her back, lifting her. When he stood with her in his arms, as if she weighed nothing, he snuggled her into his body. "I know this isn't the best time, but I'm in love with you, Bethany." He kissed her again, but this time deeply and passionately.

When he said he loved her, he felt her body tense, but as his lips met hers the tension fell away. She kissed him back, her arms wrapping around him.

* * *

"I'm sorry for your loss. We'll see they receive justice, we won't stop until Pierce has been taken down." Tabitha said, bending to give Bethany a hug. The open space of Ty's quarters left Bethany feeling exposed. The room had a masculine feel with soft touches that had to come from Tabitha. The deep red walls made the white and black furniture stand out, while the dark wood of the tables and television stand tied everything together.

Bethany nodded, holding tight to Raja's hand as if it was a life raft, as tears threatened to fall. *I will not cry again.*

"Let's get this over with. Bethany needs to get her leg elevated." Raja announced, using his free hand to wheel her toward the couch where Ty and Felix stood.

"What's this all about? If you're concerned that I'll tell your secret when I leave, there's no need. Raja saved my life and keeping his secret is the least I can do." Bethany ran her sweaty palm over her thigh.

"That's not what worries us. We're more distressed for you and your loss. We understand you wish to travel to Virginia." Ty stood next to the couch, his arm around his mate. Even entangled with his mate, he still held an air of danger and foreboding.

"Yes. I'm the only one left and would need to make arrangements."

"Bethany, I know this is hard right now, and the last thing you need is another shock." Ty slipped his arm from his mate and came around the couch to stand close to Bethany. "I would like to send in a team of shifters to search for evidence to help us locate Pierce."

"I'm sure the police will handle that." She shook her head, unable—unwilling to understand the reason behind it.

"They'll miss things. Not because they are inadequate but because they don't have the abilities we do. Shifters can pick up his scent, and track him. The police won't be able to give you the justice that you deserve."

"I doubt you could arrive before someone contacts the police." It was a feeble argument, but she barely comprehended the death of her entire family, and now this?

"Not from here, most likely. However, there's a clan in West Virginia. The Alpha and some of his best guards are already on their way."

"You were going to do it with or without my consent, is that it?" Her voice was low, but anger roused beneath the grief in her belly.

"We were hoping to gain your permission." Tabitha moved to stand next to him, gently rubbing her arm across his lower back before he encircled her in his arms.

"That doesn't answer my question."

"You're right—it doesn't." Ty smiled. "I can't give you a direct answer. Yes, the men would have checked the outside of the home to see if they were able to detect a scent. If they felt it was imperative to go inside, then yes, the order would have been given to do what was necessary."

Bethany stared at him, unsure of what to say. She appreciated his honesty, yet he informed her as what, a matter of courtesy?

"You have to understand this is about more than just you. More innocents will be killed unless he's caught. Do you really want their deaths on your conscience?"

A soft growl came from Raja and he placed his other hand on her shoulder. She shook her head. "I don't want to see anyone else die at his hands, but I would also hate for your men to go to jail for destroying evidence. Do whatever is necessary."

Ty nodded to Felix, who stepped away from the group and pulled out his cell phone.

A teakettle whistled from the kitchen. Tabitha smiled. "Adam is making us hot cocoa. I thought it would be better for you than coffee with your medication. I always enjoyed cocoa on cold winter nights."

"Thank you." Bethany didn't care about cocoa—she wanted this over. She wanted to be alone with Raja again, to be cuddled up on a couch, or better yet in bed, with his arms around him. She wanted to feel his body against hers, her hands on his chest. She was drawn to him as a heroin addict is drawn to the next needle. His touch was all she desired; she wanted it to help her forget her loss. She wished she could look at him, but that meant he would have to move—and the potent desire to stay in his arms wouldn't leave her.

"I asked Raja to speak with you about your uncle. I'm assuming he did." Tabitha's gaze went from Bethany to Raja, who was still standing behind her.

"Yes. I don't understand what my uncle has to do with any of this. So he's mentioned in the video. What does that matter? Anyone could search my family tree and find out my father had a brother."

"He wasn't just mentioned..." Ty eyed Raja. "Pierce said, 'Tonight the family will have to face the beast their uncle created.' That's the only lead we have to go on. It might answer why this happened to you."

"What would my Uncle James have to do with any of this?"

"I don't know," Tabitha said as Adam brought in a tray with cocoa and cookies. He placed it on the coffee table. "Thank you, Adam." Tabitha made her way back to the couch across from Bethany and Raja, her hand still in Ty's, making sure he followed her.

Tabitha scooted toward the edge of the couch, grabbing her mug and a freshly baked chocolate chip cookie. "Raja, will you please hand a mug to Bethany and help yourself?" She took a sip of her cocoa with eyes closed. "Tell me about your uncle."

"I don't know much. Dad always said Uncle James was a loner. He didn't like to be around people." She took the mug from Raja and held it. The warmth felt good in her hands.

"Any idea why?"

"No. I haven't seen him since I was a child."

"When I told you what I was, you mentioned your father spoke of shifters before," Raja said gently, rubbing her shoulder.

"Yeah. He told us bedtime stories about shifters growing up. He said shifters—well he didn't use that exact word—existed, and one day I would find out for myself. I never believed him until you." She reached up, placed her hand over his again and squeezed gently. "How did he know?"

"I suspect your uncle might be a shifter." Ty knelt before her, as though doing his best to break the information gently.

Bethany eyed Ty, wondering if she heard him right. *My Uncle James a shifter? Nah.* "I don't think so. My father wasn't, and they were full-blooded brothers."

"If one parent is a shifter and the other isn't, there is a fifty-fifty chance the first child will be. From there, the odds go down with each child. Who is older?"

"Uncle James."

"It's possible your uncle is a shifter and the active gene wasn't passed to your father," Raja said to her before turning his attention to Ty. "I'd like to ask Connor to search for her uncle. It's possible he's in danger."

Ty nodded. "Go ahead."

Bethany raised her hand, interrupting. "Wait a damn second. What the hell do you mean he's a shifter? Does that mean I'm one as well?"

"No. In order to be a shifter, one of your parents would had to have been a shifter. You still carry the recessive genes, but you'll never shift." Raja explained.

She sat there dumbfound. How could all this be in her family tree and yet her father have never told her.

"There's one more thing we would like to discuss with Bethany before she goes."

"I'll wait. Connor can get started once you're done here."

No one argued with him, but the tension in the room rose. Behind her, Raja went still.

Ty didn't mince his words. "We'd like to have your family's bodies sent here…"

"You what?" Bethany shouted. If she could have stood, she would have jumped out of her seat with anger.

"Please hear him out," Tabitha begged.

"I thought I wasn't a prisoner here. I told you I wouldn't share your secret. What more do you want from me?"

"We haven't lied to you. This is to protect you."

She glared at Tabitha, hatred pouring off her in waves.

"Pierce is expecting you to return home, grief-stricken and injured. You would be easy prey. We can't guarantee your safety in Virginia. We can give your family the proper ceremony here and still keep you safe."

Bethany sat in shock, shaking her head. "You knew about this?" She demanded of Raja in a whisper.

He stepped to the side of the wheelchair, and knelt beside her. "Tabitha briefly mentioned it. I wasn't aware of details. I know it's a shock, but think about it. It would keep you safe here with me to protect you. You don't stand a chance against Pierce, especially in your condition." Raja whispered.

"What about family and friends? How would I explain it?"

"You could explain that your parents didn't want a memorial service. The one here would be kept quiet. An announcement in the papers would need to be made for your family, and loose ends would need to be dealt with, but we can help you," Ty explained.

"My family wanted to be cremated, my parents' ashes buried together once they passed," her voice full of unshed tears.

"Whatever arrangements you want can be arranged here. You can save your family ashes until you find the spot you wish to bury them. We're not doing this to punish you for knowing our secret— we're trying to protect you. Your parents wouldn't want you to die." Ty leaned forward, resting his elbows on his knees.

"I understand. This is all too much. I'll need my cell phone in order for the police to reach me. Only my family knew I was in Alaska, and even if they found out where I was, they would expect me to be at the hotel, not here. I want to rest now, if that is all."

"I have it." Raja patted his pocket. "She'll be in my quarters if there is anything else. I'll let you know when the call comes through."

"Very well. I'll let you know when we hear from the West Virginia Alpha," Ty promised as Raja wheeled her toward the door.

Chapter Sixteen

"Are you comfortable?" Raja asked as he pulled the blanket up from the bottom of the bed.

"This is your room, isn't it?" She nodded.

"Yes. The guest bed isn't made, and I wanted to get you comfortable." He brushed hair away from her face. "You need to get some sleep."

"I'm not tired." She yawned. "Maybe if I give myself up to Pierce, he would kill me quickly and you could trap him. Then he wouldn't be able to kill anyone else."

"Don't even speak like that." He sat on the edge of the bed. "You won't sacrifice yourself. We will catch him."

"But…"

"He wouldn't do it quickly."

"You don't know that." She twirled her finger around the sheet.

"Trust me, I know." He growled.

She watched him closely. "How do you know?"

He pushed off the bed to pace the room that seemed to be closing in around him.

"Answer me, Raja."

"There was nothing quick about what he did to your sister." He hated telling her. "I don't want to see the same thing happen to you."

She cringed and sank deep into the mattress. The stink of her fear filled the room and grabbed his tiger's attention. "I'm sorry, Bethany." He stepped back to the bed and took her hand in his. "I shouldn't have said that."

"He tortured her," Her voice raw with fresh agony.

He crawled into bed next to her. "I'm sorry, love. I won't let anything happened to you." He whispered, holding her close. He kissed the top of her head.

"My baby sister…oh poor Jamie," she sobbed and Raja held her.

* * *

Raja pressed his cell to his ear. He slipped out of the room while Bethany slept. He had to talk to Connor.

"Connor, could you come to my quarters? I need to speak with you." Raja closed the bedroom door behind him.

When Connor agreed, he ended the call and clipped the phone back on his jeans. He booted up his laptop setting it on the coffee table before making his way to the kitchen for another cup of coffee. *Coffee won't sustain me much longer. I'm going to need to get some sleep soon if I'm going to be of any use to Bethany and the clan.*

Knowing it would be a long night, he turned on a pot of coffee when he returned. He poured the coffee in his mug, the aroma gave his mind the jerk it needed but wasn't enough to keep his eyes more than half open.

He stood, mug in hand, looking out onto the compound. A few of the clan children were having a snowball fight in the courtyard of the main building. The fluffy white snow flew through the air, as children dived out of the way, laughing. Finding Bethany had made him more aware of what a dangerous time it was for tiger shifters. He had the obligation to protect not only the clan members but more importantly Tabitha and now Bethany.

His senses were open to allow him to smell the wolf, Connor, coming down the hall. He didn't want Connor's knock to wake Bethany. Rest was the best thing for her, and it gave him time to deal with Connor. If anyone could find her uncle, it's Connor.

Coffee in hand, Raja opened the door. "Thank you for coming. Can I offer you some coffee?"

"No, thanks." Connor, a true computer geek with his light brown hair messy from running his hand through it, his ruffled dress shirt and jeans looked as if he slept in it, stood there looking ill at ease.

"Come sit down," Raja said, moving away from the door toward the sitting area. "I have a task for you."

"Whatever I can do to help." Connor took a seat on one of the chairs.

"My mate, Bethany, has an uncle. We believe he either is a key to all of this or is in danger. We need you to locate him."

Connor nodded. "I remember he was mentioned in the video. Monitoring the transmissions coming from Pierce's camp I've never heard any mention of him. Do you think he could have been the one who bit Pierce?"

"It's unlikely. Rogue shifters are normally the ones at fault. The uncle doesn't seem like a rogue, but my guess is he might know who did it."

"I understand. What information do we have to go on?"

"Very little, unfortunately. Bethany hasn't seen the man since she was a child. Her father said he was a loner and had a cabin in North Dakota. His name is James Thompson."

"I'll get to work and let you know when I find anything." Connor stood.

Raja nodded, too tired to stand, his eyes heavier than before he had the coffee. Connor shut the door and Raja set his mug aside. Resting his head on the back of the couch, he let his eyes close.

Bethany's hotel room. When the call comes in, I'll have Shadow go to the hotel and get Bethany's things, check out, and make it look like she's going to Virginia. Maybe Pierce will fall for the trap and the West Virginia clan can catch him.

He hit Ty's number and told him the plan. He could contact Lukas's brother Jinx and start putting things in motion. With that done, he slept.

Chapter Seventeen

The sun shining through the curtains woke Raja. He found himself tightly holding Bethany, his gun digging into his side, and still in the same clothes from the day before. Memories flooded back to him. In the middle of the night, Bethany had cried out for her sister Jamie, tearing at his heart. He went to her, crawled into bed and wrapped his arms around her, trying to bring some comfort.

He eased off the bed, careful not to disturb her.

"Where are you going?" Bethany asked, her voice deep with sleep, holding tightly to him.

"My gun…it's digging in."

"Take it off. Please stay with me. I need you."

"Shh, love." He ran his thumb over her cheek. "I'm not going anywhere. There's nowhere I'd rather be than right here with you in my arms."

He slipped his gun out of the holster, and set it on the nightstand in easy reach. Most of the guards carried guns even if they could shift back and forth at will. It saved any embarrassing situations that could arise from someone seeing a tiger roaming free, and the naked moments after they changed back.

The bright pink cell phone next to the gun rang. His stomach sank. This most likely was the news they were dreading, informing her of her family's demise.

"There's no need for you to do this. I can handle this for you." He closed his hand around the cell; they both already knew who called…the Virginia police.

Beside him, she nodded, and he hit the talk button.

"This is Bethany Thompson's phone. Who is this?" Raja sat on the edge of the bed, grateful for Bethany's human hearing and hoping it was enough distance to avoid her hearing any of the details about their murders.

"Detective Davis with the Virginia State Police."

"Detective Davis, I'm sorry. She is unavailable at the moment. I'm Bethany's fiancé, Raja. What can I do for you?" Out of the corner of his eye he could see surprise on her face when he said fiancé.

"My information shows Ms. Thompson is travelling, is that correct?

"She's in Alaska with me. I'm not sure what this has to do with anything. What is the nature of your call?"

"There's been an incident tonight in Virginia and I'm calling to make notification to Ms. Thompson."

"She had a snowboarding accident and has just come out of surgery, she's unavailable to take phone calls. What sort of incident are we talking about, Detective?"

"I'm sorry to have to inform you, her parents and sisters were found in their home tonight. Based on their condition—we have opened an investigation."

He rose and paced to the window as Detective Davis went over some of the details of her families murders, making the video play in his mind again. They knew it was coming yet hearing the words from the detective made it seem real. It left a sick feeling in his stomach. *Will more people die at Pierce's hands before we can take him out?*

"There must be a mistake. Why would anyone want to do that to the Thompson's? Did you catch whoever did this?" Raja didn't have to feign shock or horror, but he played it up for the officer.

"The person responsible is still at large, but we have officers following up on call tips, as well as doing a door to door canvas."

"Find the person responsible. When Bethany wakes we'll discuss arrangements and call you back. But since her family wanted to be cremated and the services held here, I don't see any reason that Bethany would need to return. Any paperwork that needs to be signed can be faxed, or dealt with through my lawyer."

The detective apologized again.

"Thank you. We will be in touch shortly with arrangements."

He ended the call and went to his now weeping mate.

"I kept hoping it was a nightmare," she whispered, her voice raw and husky from sleep and too many shed tears.

"I'm sorry, my love. I'd take away your pain if I could." He wrapped his arms around her.

"I'm alone now. I have no one."

He leaned back, prying her from his chest. "You have me. I'm not going anywhere."

"You only feel sympathy for me because I'm injured and my family was murdered. I don't need your pity."

"I'm in love with you. Sure, I have empathy for what happened to your family, but I've been falling in love with you since I first laid eyes on you." He rubbed her back, trying his best to soothe her. "You're the woman I love."

This only made her cry harder, sobs shaking her body.

"What's wrong? What did I say?"

"Why now? The timing is all wrong." She dissolved into an almost soundless cry, as if the grief straining to get out couldn't.

"I know the timing could have been better but I have you now, and I'm not going to let you go." Pulling her close, he tucked his chin against her hair and held her. He'd hold her for as long as it took.

* * *

"Raja!"

"In here." He called. He'd expected his sister Tora since Doc came to check on Bethany earlier in the day. He mentioned Tora wanted to meet Bethany.

Tora breezed into the kitchen with Scarlet happily bouncing on her hip. "Here, go visit Uncle Raja for a bit." She passed the bundle of joy off.

"How's my favorite girl?" He asked Scarlet, kissing her check. Holding his niece chased away the grief and loss from the last few days.

She snuggled her small body against his chest. When Scarlet started to purr, Bethany inhaled deeply, reminding him she wasn't used to shifters.

"Don't mind her. Shifter children tend to allow their animal nature to come through. They don't understand yet that it's unsafe. That's why the children rarely, if ever, leave the compound. We have a certified teacher here to educate the children as well," Tora said, sitting down at the table across from Bethany in Raja's empty chair.

"Tora, did you stop by for a reason or just to pawn your daughter off on someone?" He reached into the fridge for the root beer his sister favored. *I never understood how she could drink this crap. She had better be glad I love her, or I wouldn't keep it on hand for times like this.*

"I came to see the woman my big brother mated. I never thought I'd see the day…" She stopped mid-sentence when Raja turned, shooting her an angry look.

"The woman he mated with?"

"Umm…you didn't…"

"Not yet, Tora. I thought she went through enough in the last few days," Raja growled, making Scarlet become alert and her body stiff. He rubbed Scarlet's back to soothe her again.

"I'm sorry," Tora explained as she cracked the tab of her root beer.

"Someone tell me what the heck is going on? What do you mean mated?"

"I think I should make my exit now. Come on, sweetie, we'll leave Uncle Raja alone." She reached for Scarlet. "Welcome to the family. I'm sure we're going to be great friends when you forgive me for the bomb I just dropped."

Tora strolled out of the kitchen before Raja could wrap his mind around how his sister always did it. She took a simple situation and made it a disaster. Bethany sat there glaring at him, waiting for him to explain.

"More to drink?" She wasn't going to forget what Tora said, but still he gave it a shot.

"Don't even try it. Mated?"

"It's a term shifters use." Raja plopped down in the kitchen chair. Defeated, he let out a sigh. "Shifters don't date like ordinary people. We have mates. Our tigers know who they are, even when we don't want to admit it. Unusual things happen when we find our mate."

"Unusual things?"

"Things like this." He touched her hand, and focused on relieving her pain.

"My pain..." she said, touching her knee.

"Is gone...I know. My touch will relieve your pain. As your mate I can feel your emotions and pain as if it's my own."

"But mating isn't that supposed to be sexual? It sounds sexual."

"Oh it will be." He chuckled. "With everything you have gone through and your injuries, I won't rush you. I desire to make you mine, the tiger in me wants to claim you completely, but I'm trying to give you the time you need."

"Could someone else claim me as a mate in the meantime?"

He shook his head. "We believe shifters only have one mate. Plus my scent is on you. No one in their right mind would try to claim you. It would be seen as a direct challenge to my authority."

"Your authority? Over me?"

"I'm Ty's Lieutenant, second in command. It would be a challenge to my position within the clan."

"What happens when there's a challenge?"

"You fight to the death or until one submits. With Ty and my positions, it's a fight to the death. You can't have the old Alpha or Lieutenant around if you want to take over the clan." To him it was as if she asked about the weather outside.

"You could...die?" her voice full of sorrow.

"We all die sooner or later." He shrugged.

"How can you sit there as if it doesn't matter?"

"It's the way of life, but I have no plans to die anytime soon." He set his coffee aside and leaned across the table. "Especially now that I found a mate."

"But..."

"Love, there's nothing to worry about. Someone would only challenge if I appear weak. If I'm weak then it's their right. Clan life is survival of the fittest. I'm around for the long haul."

"What happens to your mate if you are killed?"

"It depends on the situation. If the mate is human sometimes they leave, return to their families. No matter what they decide, women are precious to us and protected at all costs. The mates can stay within the clan, protected, or join another clan if they chose."

"Wouldn't the challenger see the mate as a threat?"

"It wouldn't matter. She would still have to be treated with the same respect that is given to the woman of the clan. It's unlikely they would be seen as a threat. Few women hold positions of power. Shadow is the only female guard we have within the clan. There are a few others in different clans."

Raja's ear bud clicked to life, and his ear filled with Ty's voice. "Raja, a situation has arisen. I'm heading your way with the team."

"Acknowledged."

Chapter Eighteen

Raja cleaned the kitchen table off quickly to allow the team to gather there. With a fresh pot of coffee already brewing, he placed the last of the dishes in the dishwasher before facing Bethany again. "I'm not sure how long this will last. Do you want me to help you into the bedroom and you can rest, or to the couch and you can watch television?"

"Is that a nice way of saying I'm not welcome?"

"No. It's a nice way of saying this isn't something that would be enjoyable and if I were you, I would scram." He snorted. "When situations arise like this, they're not for the faint of heart. I'm sure it's not anything you need to deal with."

"But if I wanted to stay?" She still sat at the kitchen table, watching him.

"Then you're more than welcome."

"Do you think Ty will feel the same way?"

"He would have asked me to his quarters or to the conference room if he was concerned with you hearing anything. Plus, as the mate of the Lieutenant of the Alaskan Tigers you are always welcomed at the Elder meetings." He went to her, putting his hand on her shoulder. "I wasn't trying to get rid of you, as if you were unwanted, but was thinking of everything you have been through. I was trying to shelter and protect you."

He heard the door in the living room open. Ty hollered, "It's us."

"In the kitchen," he called before bending down to kiss her. "It's up to you, love."

Ty entered the kitchen followed by Tabitha, Felix, Adam and Connor, each with an expression of gloom. Tabitha looked as if she struggled the most, Ty holding securely to her, but still agony was clear on her face.

"Bethany, you're more than welcome to stay for this meeting, but if you wish to rest, Raja can fill you in later." Ty took a seat at the end of the table, pulling Tabitha into his lap and wrapping his arms around her.

"I'd like to stay and help in any way I can."

Ty nodded while the rest of the men took their seats at the table. Adam stood close to the doorway, while Raja took the last seat next to her.

"What's going on? Tabitha, are you all right?" Raja's gaze was on Tabitha, studying her.

"The change is close. I pleaded for her to stay in bed, rest, but she wouldn't listen," Ty explained as Tabitha rested her head against his chest.

"Your touch makes it bearable," she whispered, her eyes closing as her face scrunched with anguish.

"I know, babe." He stroked her arm with misery in his eyes. "Connor."

Connor nodded. "We found James Thompson. He still has the cabin in North Dakota, and it's his permanent residence according to the records. Your suspicions are true—he's a shifter."

"Okay. Send a team there. Bring him back if possible." *I hope he has answers we need.*

"I researched him, and I think you might have a better chance at getting what you want if you contact him directly. It's possible he would come to Bethany if she asked. It would be received better coming from her than a team sent to return with him."

"I think he's right. Uncle James might be more forthcoming if I contacted him. Connor, were you able to locate a phone number for him?"

"Yes." He slid her a printed piece of paper. "This is all the information I was able to find of him."

"Thank you."

"We'll contact him after the meeting." Raja reached back to grab the pot of coffee that finished brewing. The mugs already sat on the table for anyone who wanted coffee.

"Small thing down, bigger problems still to go. Your turn, Felix."

"We received another video from Pierce…"

Bethany gasped, squeezing Raja's hand. He placed his arm around her, pushing his chair closer to her.

"It was addressed to Jessica. He desires to see his sister." Felix poured himself a cup of coffee before pouring one for Ty, who still had his arms around his mate.

"Why?" Raja could feel the tension growing in Bethany. They were all thinking the same thing—had Pierce attacked again?

"I'm assuming that he wishes to gain information from her." Felix stirred sugar into his coffee cup before looking back up at Raja.

"Do you think she would betray us, especially after the last video?" Raja rubbed his thumb over the back of Bethany's hand.

"I don't think she would do it willingly. We all know he has ways to gather information when he wants it. I'd rather not risk it." Ty looked troubled, but continued rubbing Tabitha's arm—whether to soothe himself or his mate remained to be seen.

"Agreed. What does she have to say about it?"

"She believes she could get him to surrender." Felix snorted. "She's still in denial about what he is."

"His sister is here? She's one of you?" Bethany inquired.

"She's here, but she isn't a shifter. We sent Connor and Leo to bring her here, expecting she would bring some insight into Pierce."

"You aren't concerned she will betray you, giving him the location of the compound or your plans?" Bethany asked, and Raja could tell by the way her body tensed, she was concerned that Pierce might attack the compound.

"They flew straight into the compound. We have a small runway here. She wouldn't know the location. Not that it matters since Pierce's men already attacked the compound shortly after Tabitha arrived. She might still be in denial, but in her heart she knows what he is." Ty explained.

"Something isn't right…I don't feel very well." Tabitha moaned, grabbing her stomach.

"It's all right, Tabby. Don't fight it." Ty brushed his mate's hair from her face. "She's burning up. Felix, get Doc."

"Maybe she would be more comfortable on the couch." Raja went to the sink and ran the dishtowel under cool water for Ty to wipe Tabitha's head.

Ty nodded, lifting her into his arms.

"What's happening?" Bethany stood, using her crutches to keep her weight off her injured knee.

"Tabitha's completing the change and will shift for the first time soon. The first time can be painful as your body makes the necessary transitions," following Ty into the living room with the wet rag, he explained.

Ty lowered her to the couch and used the rag to wipe her face. Her body started shaking uncontrollably as if she was having a seizure. "Raja."

He went to them, grabbing Tabitha's flailing legs, as she screamed in torment. "Where the hell is Doc?"

"Don't fight it, Tabby. You're strong—you can do this." Ty held her to the couch. "I need more hands."

Connor stepped forward. "Not you, Connor." When a grief-stricken look showed on his face, Ty continued, "Your wolf might spook her tiger."

Adam waited by the door, and Felix went in search of Doc, leaving Bethany the closest. She tossed her crutches aside and balanced herself, placing the majority of her weight on her uninjured knee.

"Hold her head."

She finally got a good grip on Tabitha's head when Doc dashed through the door. "What did you do to my patient? I saw her this morning."

"Things have steadily gotten worse throughout the day until she bent over with stomach pains. We were meeting with Raja to go over some things. We brought her in here when this started. Help her," Ty growled.

"I can ease the pain, but that's it." Doc placed his bag next to the couch.

"What do you mean, that's it?"

"She has started the change. If I stop it now, it will be worse next time." He pulled out a syringe. "This will help the pain."

"What's happening to her, Doc?" Raja had a firm grip on her legs.

"It is rare, but her body has transitioned faster than expected. Her tiger wants out, but her body isn't ready. What should take a few more days is happening before our eyes," Doc readied a syringe with the drug. "Bethany, let go of her head. I need you to help me with her arm."

Doc took hold of Tabitha's flailing arm, holding it straight out. "Hold it still like this. If I don't get the vein, it will take longer to work." Bethany took hold of the arm while he tied it off, making the vein stand at attention. "Hang in there, Tabitha. This will help."

Tabitha roared as Doc pushed the needle in and the plunger down. Slowly the violent moments of her limbs gave way to shakes and then tremors. Bethany's legs shook as she reached for her crutches. Unable to reach them before her legs buckled. Raja was there to catch her before she could land in a heap, hurting her knee more.

"Will she be all right now?" Bethany whispered, voice tense with fresh pain and Raja placed her in the chair closest to the couch.

"She still has to make the transition. It shouldn't be long now. She'll have to stay here until the transition is complete. We can't risk moving her," Doc said, closing his bag.

"Connor, I'd suggest you leave. The transition could bring your wolf and we need you to trace the last video." Ty sat on the couch, Tabitha's hands in his.

"Yes, sir."

"Adam, stand guard at the door. No one is allowed in."

"Why don't you let me look at your knee while I'm here?" Doc knelt before Bethany.

"It's fine."

"You're in pain."

Raja could feel the pain. *She did it to help Tabitha. What a woman I found as a mate.* He placed his hand over hers. "Let him look at it."

"He should be worried about Tabitha."

"I got Tabby. Let him look at your knee. I'd hate to know you did more damage to it helping my Tabby." Ty nodded at her.

Doc was examining Bethany's knee when Raja felt the hairs on the back of his neck stand up. Tabitha called the magic forth, bringing on the change.

"We should have cleared the building," Raja said, looking at Ty, who nodded in agreement.

"Too late now."

The room filled with energy, as Tabitha's soft moans turned into purrs. Hair started to grow over her skin.

"Get her on the floor, if you can. It will give her more room to shift," Doc said, pushing the coffee table out of the way while Raja and Ty slid her to the floor.

"Don't fight it, embrace your tiger." Ty knelt beside his mate, who now lay on her stomach.

Her hands became paws as her body grew, her stunning strawberry fur mixing nicely with white stripes across her back. She rose to stand on her newly acquired paws and roared.

"Do you think that means she likes her new form?" Ty joked.

Tabitha tried to take a step and toppled over.

"It's from the drugs I gave her. It should work its way through her system in a few moments now that she's a tiger. Then she'll be able to shift back when she's ready."

Tabitha lay there contentedly licking her paw, observing everyone with her big blue cat eyes.

Once Tabitha rested comfortably, Raja turned his attention back to Bethany and her knee.

Chapter Nineteen

"We have to trust your uncle isn't involved with Pierce. Be up front with him but don't give him too much information over the phone. Our end is secure, but we cannot be sure his line isn't tapped. We need him to come to us." Ty sat on the couch with his sleeping mate's head in his lap. After shifting back to human form, she fell asleep. Doc thought it was from the stress of the situation and the leftover medication. She had on Ty's dress shirt since her clothes were ruined, and a blanket covered her.

"I understand." Bethany twisted the ring on her finger, nerves getting to her. *What if Uncle James wants nothing to do with me? What if he's behind everything and working with Pierce?*

"Stalling isn't going to help your stomach. Let's do this. I'll be right here with you." Raja squeezed her hand as he grabbed the phone. He dialed the number and placed the call on speakerphone, allowing everyone to hear it.

He isn't home. The phone rang and rang before someone answered. "Hello?" A rough voice came through the speaker.

"Is this James Thompson?" Raja asked.

"Who's asking?"

"My name is Raja Harrison. I'm here with your niece, Bethany…"

"Bethany—is she all right?" He cut Raja off.

"Uncle James?" The words felt strange on her tongue. *I haven't seen this man in over fifteen years.*

"Oh, child. I heard what happened to your parents and little Jamie. I was afraid they got you too. Where are you?"

"I'm safe. Do you know what happened?"

"I'm afraid I know who is behind it, yes. I can't tell you over the phone. You must come to me. I know somewhere that you'll be safe."

"I'm safe where I am. Uncle James, did you have anything to do with what happened to Mom, Dad and Jamie?"

He sighed. "I know I haven't been in your life, but how could you think I could murder my own brother and his family?" There was no anger in his voice, only disappointment.

"I didn't think you could, but I had to ask. Uncle James, I need answers."

"I know you do, child, but I can't give them to you over the phone. It's not safe."

"If you're truthful in what you say, I can arrange for you to see Bethany. But if you try to harm Bethany or us, it will be seen as a threat and will be handled as so. I'm sure you're aware of our laws." Raja spoke while rubbing her leg.

"I mean her no harm. She's the last family I have left. I want her protected. I don't want to see what happened to my brother and his family happen to her."

"Very well. You're correct—it isn't secure, so no details. Be ready." Raja ended the call.

"I don't believe he had anything to do with it." Ty ran his hand run through Tabitha's hair.

"I agree. I'll get the pilot and a team to his location straightaway. Might I borrow Adam to accompany Leo? I need to send Shadow and Thomas to the hotel to collect Bethany's things and check her out."

"Very well. One last thing then we'll take our leave, and you can put the plans into motion."

"Jinx and his team found a trail. They're following it. Are you still planning to contact the detective to make arrangements for the family?"

"Yes. I expect he's gone for the night, but the message and arrangements will be waiting for him. We'll send the plane and an escort the day after tomorrow. That will give them the time needed to complete their tasks. I've asked Tora to put together a small memorial service for the family."

Tears sprang to Bethany's eyes. "Aww Raja. That's wonderful of you but you didn't have to. None of you knew my family."

"It doesn't matter that we didn't know them. You're Raja's mate and that makes you and them family." Ty stated flatly, with such simplicity that she accepted it as a fact. "Send Lance as an escort. With his latest blunder he's off guard duty and needs something to occupy his time. With that, I'll get my mate into her own bed." He lifted Tabitha, wrapping the blanket securely around her. "I'll have Felix bring the blanket back."

* * *

"Jessica wishes to speak with you." Shadow placed Bethany's suitcase next to the couch.

"What does she want?" Raja looked over at her.

"Adam didn't say. He only asked me to tell you that she urgently wishes to speak with you. I saw him as they were gearing up for North Dakota."

"She'll have to wait. I'm can't leave Bethany alone."

"I can manage on my own if there's something that needs your attention." Bethany hobbled into the living room, freshly changed into a pair of pajamas that Tabitha brought over for her.

"I'm not leaving you." His teeth set.

"I can try to find out what she wanted, but she's insisting that she speak with you or Ty. I would prefer not to disturb Ty if possible." Shadow stood close to the door, unmoving.

"Fine, escort her here. Bethany I'd like you to remain in the bedroom while she's here."

"Why?" She made it to the couch and was about to sit and prop her knee up as Doc instructed her.

"She's the one that received the video about your family. She knows what happened to you. I'm not sure she's ready to face you yet." He also didn't want Bethany to have to deal with Jessica; she didn't need to see the sister of the man who tried to have her killed. Raja watched as Shadow eased out the door. Obviously she didn't want to get involved.

"You're concerned that she'll what? Try to kill me like her brother?"

"No. I told you she's in denial. I'm not sure she wants to face proof of it yet."

"Well ready or not she's about to." Bethany lowered herself to the couch and tossed a pillow under her knee. "I'm not going to hide in the bedroom like some scared chick. Maybe seeing me will shake her out of her denial."

"Or maybe not."

"If it doesn't then you're no worse off than you are now."

He threw his hands up in the air, unwilling to fight. Or possibly his subconscious knew she was right. Either way she won this round. *Is this what mating is like? Giving in to a woman?*

"You're twisting me around your little finger just as Scarlet does. Am I that easy?"

"You want to make the people you care about happy. You hate to see sadness or pain in them. Therefore, you do whatever you can to avoid it. But no, you're not easy. You're an honorable, loving man. I don't know how I managed to catch such a man. You've been my rock through all of this."

He grabbed another throw pillow, grateful to his sister for insisting on them, and used it to prop her knee higher. "I'm glad I'm not transparent. Scoot down. Let me sit behind you with my arms around you, and you can still have your leg on the couch. I want to feel your body next to mine."

She did as he asked, and he slipped behind her, pulling her close to him, his arm around her as she rested her head on his shoulder. "Comfortable?"

"Umm...Raja, why haven't you completed the mating?"

"You have been through a lot the last few days and, with your knee, you're in pain. I'm giving you the time I thought you needed."

"I don't need time—it's you I need."

"Soon, love, soon." He buried his face in her hair, breathing in her scent. "They're coming, You sure you want to do this?"

She nodded as the door opened and in stepped the woman. Shadow keeping a close eye on Jessica but gave her the space not to feel crowded.

"Jessica, what's so important that you had to see me tonight?"

"Ahh...umm..." She eyed Bethany with pity.

"Whatever you need to say can be said in front of my mate. If you don't wish to, then Shadow can escort you back to your room."

"It's...I didn't expect her here."

"She's my mate. Now what did you want?" He repeated, unwilling to coddle the woman and her denial.

"Mate?" She shook her head. "I was going through email conversations I've had with Pierce through the years. I found a few things that might be of importance."

"What did you find?" *She's working my patience. This is like pulling teeth.*

"He mentioned a James Thompson. I don't know who it is, but I recognized the last name."

"My uncle?" Bethany whispered.

"What about him?" Raja's thoughts were turning negative quickly.

"I'm not really sure. I remember him saying it all started with James."

"Started with him how?"

"I'm not sure. After he was bitten, he said it boiled down to being James's fault. He didn't bite him but somehow he's tied into it. But in all the years since, the name never came up."

"Okay. We'll get to the bottom of how he ties into the situation at hand. Anything else?" Raja's fingers played with the edge of Bethany's pajama top.

"There's also a hunting cabin in North Dakota our parents owned. I own it now but never use it. He has a key and goes there when he needs to regroup or hide. It's probable he might be there or maybe there's a clue to where he might be."

Bethany gasped at the words North Dakota, but when Raja squeezed her arm, she said nothing.

"If that's all, Shadow will escort you to your room. Give her the address and we'll get a team to investigate it."

Chapter Twenty

"Adam and Leo are an hour out from James's location. We'll need another team for Jessica's tip. I wanted them to investigate the cabin and if he's there, wait for backup to arrive. We'll send in two teams, but more will be sent if he's there." Raja stood in Ty's living room giving him the update. Bethany was asleep in his quarters with Shadow standing guard.

Ty nodded. "I'll get the teams on it. When James arrives we need to debrief him first. Bring Bethany here—she can stay with Tabitha and her guards. I don't want the women in danger if James is tied in with Pierce. I also want Shadow with us. She'll know if we can trust him."

"I have a feeling the women aren't going to be very happy with either of us when we tell them they have to sit this one out."

"True, but it's for the best," Ty snickered.

"What's for the best?" Tabitha asked, coming out of the bedroom.

"I'll let you handle this one. I have my own to deal with." Raja turned to make a quick exit as Ty gave him a dirty look and Tabitha stood with her hands on her hips. He laughed, closing the door behind him. *Now to tell my mate.*

While he strolled through the main building back toward his quarters, he took a moment to text Adam. *Be on guard. Pierce's sister has a cabin in ND, he might be there.* With his cell phone still out he sent Tora a brief message also. *Your big mouth is going to get us in trouble one of these days.* He smiled, remembering all the times he covered for his sister. Her big mouth already landed them in some tricky situations in the past.

His cell vibrated in his hand. *She must have taken it well…you're still alive. You can thank me later.*

"Thank her? She must have lost her marbles," he mumbled, reaching his door.

He found Shadow sitting on the window seat hugging her legs. Even in the dark he couldn't miss her bright pink leggings and white and pink sweater. The pink stood out against the darkness of the room.

"Shadow, when Adam and Leo arrive with Bethany's uncle, I'd like you to attend the debriefing before I allow her to meet him. We want to make sure he has nothing to do with Pierce before we endanger her."

"Do you think it is wise to leave her alone?"

"She'll be with Tabitha and her guards while we meet James." He leaned against the back of the chair closest to her, whispering so not to disturb Bethany.

"Very well. If I might make a suggestion."

Shadow was still unsure of herself, especially around the Elders.

"You're one of our most trusted guards. You may always speak freely and give your suggestions. We might not use them, but we're always willing to listen."

She smiled a smile that didn't quite reach her eyes, but it was warm. "She needs her own guards, especially until Pierce is caught. She's in as much danger as Tabitha. He'll come after her again if he gets a chance."

"Funny you should bring that up I was considering the same thing this evening. Are you applying for the position?"

"I prefer the field, but I could be persuaded, I'm sure." Her eyes held a twinkle of excitement.

"Think it over and let me know your requirements. I'd like to have you as the Captain of her Guards if you're interested." He slid his hands into his pockets. *I thought I'd have a hard time convincing her, and here all along she was interested.*

"I'll sleep on it and let you know tomorrow." She rose, stretching her long body. "Go to your mate and rest. You both need it. I feel something bad is coming this way."

* * *

"Where were you?" Bethany whispered as he tried to sneak back into the bedroom. "Why are you dressed?"

"I had to meet with Ty." He slipped his gun holster and knife off and laid them on the nightstand.

"Why didn't you wake me?"

"You were sleeping soundly. I had Shadow here in case you woke." He unbuttoned his shirt with her gaze on him.

"You should have woken me."

"And what? Dragged you with me? You needed the sleep. You were safe here with Shadow, and I was just down the hall." He tossed his shirt aside, moving his hands to his belt. "Plus what I spoke with Ty about wasn't something you had to be there for. We were discussing sending teams to locate Jessica's cabin."

"You're right. Sleep was better." She smiled at him. "Now are you coming to bed?"

"If you want me to."

"Oh yes. I want you to." She eagerly slid over, giving him more room to join her on the bed. *I want all of you. I hunger to feel your hands on me.*

He slipped his jeans off, letting them fall to the floor. The moonlight reflected off his toned, muscular body, as he stood before her in only his boxers. His black, shoulder-length hair cascading around his face, and desire flickered in his piercing green eyes.

"Come here," she whispered, almost raw with need. She lifted the blanket, inviting him.

He slipped under the covers with her. Lying on his side with his arm propped under him; he studied her.

"What?"

"You're beautiful." He played his fingers lightly on her arm.

"I want you." Her cheeks heated with embarrassment with her sudden outburst.

"We should wait. Give your knee time to start the healing process."

"I don't want to wait. My knee will be fine as long as we're careful. Don't make me wait, Raja. I need to feel your hands on me." She leaned her head forward, bringing their lips close. "Please."

Her lips were met with the dark taste of coffee, rejuvenating her. *No wonder he tastes like coffee. He drinks as if it is his life's nectar.* His tongue teased her lips open, turning it from passionate into a deep, hungry kiss. His hand ran through her hair, keeping her close.

"Are you sure?" he asked, breaking away from the kiss, his fingers going to her nightshirt.

"I'm sure." She leaned forward, allowing him to slip the shirt over her head. "I need you."

He tossed the shirt away and kissed her neck. He rubbed his cheek against her neck, like a cat against a body.

"What are you doing?" She laughed as his hair tickled her neck.

"Marking my mate properly. I want my scent all over you. You're mine."

"Hum."

"There will be no going back from this. You'll be mine. If you have reservations, we should deal with them first." He rested his head in the hollow of her neck.

Mating. "I have no doubts when it comes to you. I love you, Raja." It didn't matter that it happened fast or the circumstances, he was the one truly *right* piece of her world.

"Good, because you're my world. I love you too." He kissed her. He slid his hand deep under the covers, gliding smoothly down her torso until he found her sweet spot. His fingers slipped between her lips, entering her core, tantalizing her with yearning.

"These must go." She hooked her hand in his boxers, and tugged.

"All in due time, my love" He winked at her. "I want to enjoy every moment, feel every inch of your body against mine."

She groaned. "You made me wait this long, and now you're going to take your time?"

"Yes," he teased with a wicked grin on his face.

"If I didn't have this damn brace on my leg, I'd roll you over and take control of the situation."

"You could try, but shifters are stronger than humans. Now lay back and let me enjoy myself, bring you pleasure, or I could draw this out longer."

With no visible choice, she leaned back against the pillows, watching the moonlight bounce off his chest. There was enough light coming through the window to allow her to see him. She had no doubt that he was able to see better than she could ever have hoped to. *Will he like what he sees? Listen to me, I'm as nervous as a virgin on her wedding night.*

"You're beautiful." He took her nipple in his mouth, sucking gently, before letting it slide out again. His cool breath made her nipple harden.

She raked her hands through his hair, moving it out of his eyes, allowing her to truly see him. She loved the feel of the silky strands of hair between her fingertips and the way his hands caressed her body.

Raja tenderly kissed her neck as he slipped two fingers inside, stroking the fire that was burning in her.

"You're wet," he whispered, his breath hot against her neck.

"Please, Raja. I need you." She turned her head to him. "Don't make me wait."

He lifted his head from her neck and met her gaze. "Please," she whispered as their lips touched. She ran her hands down his chest, feeling his tight abs on her way to his shaft. She slid her hands inside his boxers, wrapping her fingers around his hard shaft. Her hand worked his shaft, while their kisses got deeper.

"Let me." He leaned back and ripped the boxers off. The ripping sound filled the room before material was tossed to the floor to join her nightshirt. She felt her eyes get big with surprise. "What? They were in the way."

She laughed.

"Keep your leg up on the pillows, I'll work around it. I won't have you doing more damage to it." He slid between her legs, angling himself with the tip of his shaft playing lightly along her folds.

As he entered her tight channel, she cried out with pleasure. His thrust was gentle at first, working his way into her core, allowing her body to adjust around him. She relaxed around him, giving him the room he needed. His thrusts came deeper and faster.

Their bodies worked together in precision, as if it was a well-choreographed dance. Their bodies rode back and forth until they exploded in unison.

Breathless, they laid there hot and sweaty, not wanting to move, their legs still entwined together.

"I love you, Bethany," Raja whispered and buried his face in her hair.

Chapter Twenty-One

After hours of making love Raja and Bethany lay tangled in each others arms, blanketed by exhaustion as night became day. His mating couldn't have come at a worse moment. Tiger shifters were living in a dangerous time, but still he couldn't deny himself the pleasures of Bethany.

"You're thinking too hard." She draped against his side, snuggling.

"Hum?"

"When you're thinking hard, you have a deep line that forms on your forehead. Penny for your thoughts?"

"It's nothing," he whispered and kissed the top of her head.

"If we're mates, we should be straightforward with each other. A relationship that isn't built on honesty and trust isn't one I want to be in."

"I was just thinking what bad timing this mating is. It's dangerous to be a tiger shifter or someone even connected to us now, especially the Alaskan Tigers. Pierce will stop at nothing or no one."

She took it in. "Do you have control over mating?"

"No. Not really. We can hold it off for a short time, but it infuriates the tiger. It makes us on edge as we battle the tiger claws and rage. If it takes too long, our animal will take control of the mating. When that happens it's perilous—we can be uncontrollable with the need for our mate's touch."

"Then why worry about the bad timing? If there was nothing you could do, isn't it better to accept the situation?" She ran her hand lazily over his chest, caressing his abs.

"Just because you make a good point doesn't mean the worry vanishes. I'm not worried for myself, it is you I'm concerned for." He stared at the ceiling, wishing they weren't having this conversation.

"Me?"

"Yes. There are transitions that will be taking place soon, and it could...well to be honest, dangerous situations will arise from it."

"I can take care of myself. What transitions?" She propped herself up on her elbow and gazed down at him.

"Bethany, you're an amazing woman with many talents..."

"But?"

His lips curved into a smile. "But you don't stand a chance against shifters. We're stronger, faster, and deadlier than a raving human on drugs." He rubbed his thumb over the dimple in her chin. "I don't want anything to happen to you."

"I'll be fine." Lowering her head, she pressed a light kiss on his lips.

"To see to that I'm assigning guards to you. It is normal procedure with the Alpha and the Lieutenant's mates. I should have done it when you first arrived, but I was more concerned about your knee and how you would react to the news of shifters—and coming to terms with you being my mate."

"I think I've done very well. Now what transitions?"

"My persistent mate." Before he could tell her of the transitions, his cell phone vibrated on the nightstand.

Grabbing it, he saw it was a text message from Ty.

He's ten minutes out. Felix and Marcus are bringing Tabitha there. Meet me at heliport, five minutes.

"He?" she asked, looking at the phone screen.

"Tabitha will explain the transitions when she gets here. I'll be back shortly." He slipped out of bed. He strolled naked toward the closet.

"Who is he?"

"Nothing to worry about. I'll be back soon." He slipped his legs into a clean pair of black jeans then grabbed the long-sleeved t-shirt that he favored.

"Answer me." She threw a pillow at him, hitting him in the back.

"James."

"Uncle James is here already. Let me get dressed." She threw off the covers.

"I meant to tell you last night but well, we got sidetracked. Ty and I have decided to meet with him first. I'll bring him to see you after we have spoken with him." After slipping the shirt over his head, he strapped his knife to his thigh and grabbed the gun holster.

"Why can't I be there?"

"Your uncle knows something. We don't know if he's working with Pierce or not. I want you here with Tabitha and her guards until we get a read on him. I promise if he is clean, I'll bring him to you."

"How would you know he's clean?" she asked, pulling on a pair of lounge pants from the bottom of the bed. They were the easiest to wear with the knee brace.

"I'm taking Shadow with me. She has the ability to see into someone's psyche and to be able to tell if they're lying. If there is anything evil about James, she'll notice it. If he wishes to harm you or anyone here, she would see it. I'll apologize now—if he means any of us harm he'll be escorted out of the compound."

"Raja, we're here," Tabitha called, coming into his quarters.

"Make yourself at home. We'll be out in a moment." He went to Bethany, kneeling in front of her. "Don't fight me on this. I'm protecting you."

She hooked her bra, but she still needed a shirt. Her nightshirt wouldn't do to meet her uncle after all these years. "I want to see him one way to another."

"I can't promise you that. I won't put you in danger, no matter how angry you'll be at me. I can tell you I'll do my best to make you happy." He stood, grabbing one of the sweaters from her suitcase. "Here."

* * *

Raja stood at the helipad, feeling guilty. *It'll break her heart if her uncle is involved in any of this.*

"Apprehensive that James has something to do with this?" Ty asked, leaning against the railing surrounding the heliport.

"We don't know completely he doesn't."

"No, but Adam is quickly becoming an outstanding guard, or I wouldn't have added him to Tabitha's guards. He has good judgment. If he found James suspicious, he wouldn't be bringing him here. Plus neither of us thought he was part of it. You're only doubting your judgment now for dread of how it will affect your mate," he added when Raja looked guilty. "Don't worry, I do it as well when it comes to Tabby. It's only natural to want to protect your mate from harm and heartbreak. But we have to trust in our instincts. It's what keeps us and our mates alive."

"You're right." Raja ran his hand down the leg of his jeans as the first sounds of the helicopter came from the distance. "After all this I need to explain to Bethany the dangers that might be in store for shifters and their mates. Not just Pierce but also with the joining of the clans."

Ty nodded. "Make sure she doesn't tell James."

"I swear if he has anything to do with the attack on Bethany, I'll kill him myself," he growled as the helicopter came into view. Adam was at the helm, steering it toward them.

"If that is the case, he'll be all yours once we get all the information out of him." Ty stepped forward, standing straight and tall when the helicopter landed. "How long do you think we have before Felix is begging for a break from our mates? He can't be having an easy time of it with both wanting to be here."

"They were both shooting looks that could kill at me when I left them. I expect we have only a short time before they drive the guards to a breaking point. Maybe we'll go back and find them bound and gagged." They laughed as the men stepped out of the helicopter. The last man to exit had to be her uncle. He was an older man who looked to be in his mid to late fifties. *He has Bethany's green eyes.*

"Ty, Raja, this is James Thompson," Adam said, coming to stand in front of him. "James, this is the Alpha of the Alaskan Tigers, Ty and his Lieutenant, Raja."

"James, if you could follow us to the conference room."

"Where's my niece? I demand to see Bethany."

"You'll see her once we have had our discussion. She's safe, that's all that you need to concern yourself with," Raja said, irritation showing in his voice.

"I want to see her now," James complained as he followed them to the conference room, Adam and Leo taking up the rear.

"As I said you can see her once this is complete and not until then. If that doesn't suit you, you're more than welcome to get your ass back on the helicopter and they'll return you to your life. But you're on our turf and you'll do things our way." Raja growled at him.

James was a weak shifter. Raja could feel it in the air around him. Yet he had the courage of a fighter. If he had anything to do with the attack on Bethany, he would be hard to break. His commitment and honor would be strong.

"If anything has happened to my niece…"

Raja's lips curled into a snarl. Not even five minutes on the ground and he was already losing patience with James.

Ty interrupted and focused his considerable attention on Bethany's uncle. "No harm has come to her since she has arrived here. She's with my mate, and they're safe. If we could get this out of the way quickly you may see her." The Alpha opened the door to the conference area. They decided to use one of the smaller ones on the far side of the compound, farthest away from the mates.

Shadow and Thomas sat at the table waiting for them. Ty took the chair at the end, leaving the one to his right for Raja, before gesturing toward the other chairs. "Please have a seat and we can get started."

James stalked to a seat, the anger sliding off him. Raja watched him out of the corner of his eye, but his attention focused on Shadow. He watched her, waiting for some sign of her impression of James. *Was he a threat to Bethany? To the clan?*

"What do you need from me?" James sat across from Shadow at the middle of the table.

"Do you know a man named Pierce?" Ty dug through the folder lying on the table and came out with a picture of Pierce.

He slid it across the table to James, who leaned back as the picture came into view. The tension in the room inched higher. James remained still with everyone watching him closely.

"Nothing, I know nothing," James said, his eye twitching slightly.

"If you're not up front with us, you won't be able to see Bethany. We won't risk her life." Raja fought the need to stand, to pace the room.

"She's my family—you can't keep me from her."

"Want to bet?" he snarled.

"Whatever you know about Pierce might help us find him. I'm sure you want to see justice for what happened to your brother and his family. Justice for Bethany." Shadow leaned forward in her chair, her voice so low and sweet; one wouldn't have guessed her to be one of the fiercer guards.

"I do, but that's a family matter."

"It's bigger than a family matter. He has gone after my mate. He has a bounty on Bethany's head. This is bigger than you." Ty laced his fingers together and laid them on the table.

"I don't want Bethany injured or killed." He looked down at the picture again.

"Then help us."

"It began many years ago." James deflated. "I married my high school sweetheart. She had problems, split personalities mostly. I loved her and thought I could fix her. It started out fine. We had a small home near the plant I took a job at after high school. I wanted to go to college, but there wasn't enough money. My baby brother had the brains. I got a job and helped my parents, put away what I could for his college and did my best for my wife. She got pregnant within the first year of our marriage, but the pregnancy was hard on her. It brought out more personalities, meaner ones. You never knew where you stood with her, and our marriage started to suffer."

"I don't understand what this has to do with Pierce." Raja shot a questioning look at James.

"You have to understand how it started. It started with me and my wife, but it ends with Pierce." James played with his short goatee as he spoke. "Six months into the pregnancy she had a breakdown one day when I was working a double. I got the call from her sister. She was admitted to the hospital after trying to drown herself. She survived, but she was never the same. Giving birth to our son only made things worse. She wanted nothing to do with him. They wouldn't discharge her from the hospital, and eventually we transferred her to a long-term facility to receive the treatment she needed. Her younger sister moved in and helped with James Junior—J.J.—while I worked. He was seven when she married and moved away, and he was already showing signs of his instability." He paused, looking down at his hands. "When J.J. shifted, things became worse. Six months after his first shift he attacked Pierce."

"Where is J.J. now?" Shadow asked softly.

"You know our law…"

"He's dead?"

"Yes. He was my son. I took care of it. I should have acted sooner, but I never thought...I guess that's it—I never thought."

"That explains the statement in the video." Raja pushed back his chair. He couldn't sit there any longer.

"Statement? Video?"

"Pierce has taken to sending us videos of his actions. We received one when Bethany was kidnapped, and one of the murders."

"Kidnapped? You said she was safe!" James hollered, slamming his hands down on the table.

"She's safe now, because Raja went after her. The kidnapper is dead. Unfortunately, Raja wasn't able to get to her before they hurt her. Her captor took a steel pipe to her knee to ensure she wouldn't escape. When Raja brought her here, Doc performed surgery to save her knee. She's recovering and doing very well." Ty slid another photo across the table. "This is the man who kidnapped Bethany. Do you know him?"

James shook his head. "No. What's this about a statement from the video?"

"In the video Pierce said 'tonight the family will have to face the beast their uncle created.' Has Pierce made any contact with you?"

"No. I haven't heard from him. After I became aware of what J.J. did, I dealt with the issue. I went to Pierce all those years ago and tried to teach him the ways of our kind. I wanted to help him adjust. He was angry and didn't want anything to do with me. I didn't create him."

"Regrettably I believe he places the blame on you, which is why he targeted your family." Raja leaned against the wall, his hands in his pockets.

"He'll come after Bethany again." James said as more of a statement than a question.

Raja nodded. "I won't let harm come to Bethany. That's why we insisted on the meeting before reuniting you with Bethany."

"You thought…I had something to do with all this? With Pierce?"

"It was a possibility we couldn't rule out."

"And now?" James asked, fiddling with the picture on the table. "Shadow?"

"His wants match ours. He wants Bethany safe and Pierce taken care of." Shadow took one last look at James and turned around to face Raja. "His words are true. I can feel his agony for the loss of his family and the concern for Bethany."

"What's the meaning of all this?"

"Shadow here is very valuable. We're lucky to have her as a part of our clan. She can get into your psyche, she knows if someone is lying. I asked her to attend this meeting to give us a read on you. I wouldn't risk the clan or reunite Bethany with someone that will only bring her heartbreak and pain in the end." Raja pushed off the wall. "Shadow, give us ten minutes and then escort James. We'll be waiting."

Chapter Twenty-Two

"James cleared the security meeting. Shadow will bring him along in a moment, but I wanted to debrief you on the meeting first. There are a few things I believe you should be aware of and after, if you don't want to see him that's your decision." Raja sat on the couch next to his lounging mate, her hand in his, and went over what happened at the meeting.

"Uncle James is cleared? You don't suspect he had anything to do with what's happened?"

"If I doubted him for a second, he wouldn't be on his way to our quarters." Raja nodded. "He'd be out on his ass instead. Family or not."

"He's all I have left."

"You're wrong there, love." He lifted her hand to his lips, and brushed a soft kiss to her knuckles. "You have me and the Alaskan clan, not to mention my big-mouth sister."

"I like Tora." She squeezed his hand.

"Good because she is already nagging to find out when you will officially be her sister-in-law and telling me Scarlet wants cousins."

They were laughing when Shadow open the door. "May we enter?"

Raja nodded and kissed Bethany's hand again. "I'll leave you two to get reacquainted. I'll be in my office if you need me." He rose from the couch, already missing her touch. "Shadow, if you could stand guard at the door." His office was off the living room, giving the impression of privacy while still allowing him to be close if needed. He couldn't afford to lose her. His heart and soul were on the line.

* * *

"Oh Bethy." Her uncle sank into the chair across from her. "Your knee."

"Uncle James, I'm fine. It's been much too long since anyone's called me Bethy."

"Your father started that when you were a child. Oh how he adored you. You were the apple of his eye. My sympathies on your loss."

"Our loss." A fresh wave of tears filled her eyes. *He looks so much like Dad. A little greyer around the temples, but other than that I'd swear he was Dad.*

"What's going on with you and that man?"

"Raja? He saved me…"

"Don't give me that, Bethy. I'm not blind. I can see there's more than that between you. I can smell him on you. You're sitting in his living room looking as if you belong here."

"Maybe I do…Uncle James, I never believed you could fall in love with someone in such a short time, but I do. I love him." She played with a strand of hair that fell out of her ponytail. Wrapping it around her fingers, looking at the ends, a nervous habit she'd never outgrown.

"I was afraid you would say that."

"Uncle James. I don't need a lecture right now. If you don't support it, that's your right but please, I don't need this now."

"It's not that I don't support you. I hoped you would settle down with a human. Shifters can be dangerous. Did he at least explain things to you?" He propped his ankle on his knee and leaned back in the chair. His well-worn cowboy boots caught her eye. *Dad always loved cowboy boots. His were normally black and cared for, but he had an office job. He didn't have to do the hard work Uncle James did.*

"You mean mating?" At his nod, she continued. "Yes, he has told me everything. It hasn't changed my mind. I love him and want to be with him. If he asked me to marry him—if shifters even do that—tomorrow, I'd say yes in a heartbeat. I don't care that he's a shifter."

"As long as you know what's in store for you. You realize your children could be shifters as well?"

"Why haven't I seen you since I was a child?" The question slipped out before she could stop it.

"He—Raja, your mate told you what happened, about my son J.J.? After that, I withdrew, kept to myself, only venturing into town once a month for food and supplies. Your father and I exchanged letters a few times a year, but I never came to visit. Seeing him happy with his family when mine was taken from me was too hard."

"Through the years I asked about you. I missed you coming to visit, the way you would toss me into the air. Dad would tell me stories about you. He even told me about shifters, but I thought he was making it up. Fantasy stories to put me to sleep. Now I realize he wasn't."

"Bethy, I missed you more than anyone else. You were like the daughter I never had. I hope you won't push me away now that you found someone to love."

"I won't." She yawned. Her eyes grew heavy and exhaustion swamped her. "Sorry, it's been a long few days."

"Would anyone like anything to drink? I'm going to put another pot of coffee on." Raja stepped out of the office.

"Is that all you drink?" She laughed.

"It's the only thing worth drinking." He shrugged.

"Thank you, but I believe Bethy is tired. I should let her rest."

"Want me to help you into bed?" Raja asked.

She nodded, grateful for the help. Exhausted emotionally, physically and mentally, she wasn't sure she could make it to the bedroom with those damn crutches.

"I'll get her settled. Why don't you stay and have a cup of coffee with me?" Raja asked James as he scooped her into his arms.

"Uncle James, please don't leave while I'm asleep." She rested her head on Raja's chest, her eyes at half-mast.

"I'll stay as long as you want me to and your friends allow."

"Thank you."

Raja carried her from the room as she fought sleep. He kicked the door shut once in the bedroom. Then he laid her on the bed.

"Here you go, love. I'm going to talk to James for a bit then I'll check on you. If you need anything holler."

"You won't make him leave while I'm sleeping, will you?" She murmured against his neck, rapidly losing the battle to stay awake.

"No. He's welcome to stay. We'll put him up in one of the guest cabins. Now rest." He kissed her and covered her with a blanket.

* * *

Two strong black coffees set on the table between them, and silence weighed heavy in the air as the two men stared at each other.

"You mated my niece." James finally broke the silence.

"So I did."

"I don't want to see her hurt."

"Neither do I. I love her."

"But you're the Lieutenant of the Alaskan Tigers. Danger follows you."

"I am, but she'll be protected. I'm assigning guards to her. Danger follows every shifter. If anything, she'll be more protected as my mate than some shifters. Any threat against her could be seen as a threat against me, and you know what happens then."

"You would kill someone…" James's hands were around the coffee mug as it set on the table.

"It's the life of being a shifter. If it came down to it, yes I would. I'm secure in my position and will protect it and my mate to the death."

"I'm not sure if that comforts or worries me more." He raised the mug to his lips and took a drink.

"Be reassured that your niece *will* be safe; that I will protect her at all costs. Could she get that with a human? I think not. A human wouldn't be able to stand against Pierce and his men. A human wouldn't be able to keep her safe." If she'd been home with her parents—she, like her whole family, would already be dead. Raja didn't give voice to those words. The cold reality of it lived like a cancer in his belly. As horrible as her ordeal had been, he was grateful that she had been close enough for him to save.

Clearing his throat, he studied her uncle. The man had his own losses to mourn. "As a shifter you should be able to feel the love and bond between us. You heard it from her lips that she loves me." At James' look of surprise, Raja smiled faintly. "Yes, I heard that. Did you really think I was far enough away to miss even a moment? The place isn't big enough to give you that kind of privacy. In addition, you might be family, but I don't know you enough to trust that you mean no threat to me, to her, or to the clan. I won't allow you to ruin her happiness. I won't stand by idly and let anyone hurt my mate. And you would hurt her by coming between us."

"I have no desire to cause her any heartache. If she loves you, then I want her happy. But if she's hurt because of you, I won't stand by idly either." James took the last sip of his coffee before setting the mug down.

"Good. Now that we have come to an understanding, we have a guest cabin that you're more than welcome to stay in. Bethany would like you to, unless you have some other engagement that you need to return to."

"No, I told her I would stay. Thank you. I left a small suitcase in the helicopter."

"I'll have Shadow show you to the cabin. You can stop by and pick up your suitcase on the way. I'm sure Bethany would like it if you would join us for a family dinner this evening. It's at my sister Tora's house, but she won't mind an extra person and it will give you more time with Bethany."

"If you're sure Tora won't mind."

"It'll be fine. Come back here at say…eight o'clock, and we'll go together." Raja hit the ear bud communication. "Shadow."

Moments later Shadow stood in the kitchen doorway.

"Please show James to one of the guest cabins, he'll be staying with us. Then if you would return."

She nodded. "If you'd follow me, James, we can get you settled."

Chapter Twenty-Three

"Shadow, please have a seat." Raja motioned the younger shifter toward a chair. Tension kept his body taut. The lack of sleep took its toll on him. "Have you had time to think over my offer?"

"To be the Captain of Bethany's guards? Yes, I have." She sat in the black leather chair closest to the door. Her white sweater made her look small against the stark black of the leather.

When she failed to elaborate and silence stretched between them, he leaned forward. "And?" He hadn't considered secondary options if Shadow declined the position.

"I'll do it with two conditions. One, that I still have an option for fieldwork from time to time. I like being on active duty but this is an opportunity I can't pass over. I realize it's a promotion, one that might not come around again, and I like Bethany. I want to keep her safe. The second is I want a say in the other guards. I won't trust her safety to just anyone." She crossed her legs and sat back in the chair, making herself comfortable.

"We can arrange for you to have fieldwork as long as there is someone *I* trust to keep Bethany safe. As for guards, do you have anyone in mind that you would like to work with?" Pleased with her agreement, he also understood her need to assert authority over her selection.

"Styx for one. Also Drew and Jayden."

"I understand Styx is a great warrior. But Drew and Jayden, what makes them stick out from the other guards?

"I've completed numerous missions with Drew and Jayden. They're good soldiers, they take orders well and have great instincts." She leaned forward in the chair placing her elbows on her knees.

"Very well. I was also thinking Milo. He's a very experienced warrior, but since the injury he has requested time out of the field. It will offer him a new position and responsibilities, while still giving him the time he needs to recover." Raja traced his thumb down the fold of the couch arm. He carried the responsibility of that injury.

"Was it in the line of duty?" Patient curiosity gleamed in Shadow's expression.

Raja nodded, taking a deep breath before answering. "Milo and Adam accompanied me on a hunt for a rogue. It was supposed to be an easy assignment. While Milo got the human woman out safely, the rogue attacked from behind. The woman wasn't injured, but in the fight the rogue cut through the nerves of Milo's arm. Fortunately, Milo shifted after the incident, but his recovery will take time." He put his hand over his eyes, using his middle finger and thumb to rub his temples.

"If you believe he's up for the job, then so be it. I have only heard good things about him and his skills." Shadow sat back in the chair again.

"Then we have the team together. Brief them. If you wish to have a training session to make sure they'll work well together, go for it. Bethany and I will be at Tora's for dinner tonight. I don't believe she'll need guards there, but I'd like someone on call at all times."

"Understood. I appreciate the chance to lead, Raja." She rose from the chair to leave.

"You deserve it."

* * *

He held Bethany close as they snuggled in bed together. Breathing in the fresh coconut scent of her shampoo, he enjoyed the way her body felt against his. *This is what I've been missing all these years. How is it possible to fall head over paws in love with someone in such a short time? Please don't let me screw this up.*

"You're thinking too hard again. Your forehead crease is back." Bethany murmured.

"I'm thinking about how much I love you." He kissed her, drawing her lower lip between his teeth and giving it a little nip. "Shall I show you again how much I love you?"

"I can't handle any more of your loving right now. As it is, I won't be able to walk straight," she teased.

"Later then." He kissed her again. *I can never get enough of her sweet kisses.* "We should get ready. We're supposed to be at Tora's in an hour."

"I need a shower."

"Bath...Doc's orders. Unless you want me to shower with you. You have to keep your weight off your knee for a bit longer."

"A bath it is then, because if you shower with me we'll be late."

He kissed her check. "I'll run the water, then I need more coffee. Want some?" Not waiting for her reply, he slid out of the bed and went to run the water for her bath. He'd still hear her.

"No thanks. My nerves are jumpy enough without adding caffeine into the mix. Do you drink anything besides coffee?"

"It's the liquid of the gods, a gift from heaven. To drink anything else is a sin." He made it back into the bedroom in time to see her roll her eyes at him and laugh. Even her playful expressions filled him with joy. "Need help into the tub? You'll need to keep your leg out of the water, so I put some towels on the edge that you can rest it on."

"I'm fine. Go drink your gift from the gods."

Chapter Twenty-Four

An hour later James, Bethany and Raja stood in Tora's country cabin living room. The oversized stone fireplace dominated the wall, with a large screen television mounted above. The hardwood floors gleamed as if they were in a showroom, while the rest of the house had that lived in look. Scarlet's toys cluttered the floor, with a rocking pony sitting next to the fireplace. A large, worn throw rug lay in front of the hearth, making the area inviting.

"Please make yourself at home." Tora told James as she leaned in to hug Bethany. Then she laid a kiss on her brother's cheek. "You're in time to read Scarlet a bedtime story. I fed her early so we could have an adult dinner tonight. Bethany, why don't you join me in the kitchen? James, you're more than welcome to join us or Marcus on the deck. He's grilling the steaks."

What does she have up her sleeve? Raja eyed his sister with uncertainty. "Come on, James, I'll introduce you to my brother-in-law."

* * *

Bethany sat at the kitchen table, her leg stretched out on the chair across from her. Compared to the living room, the kitchen was ultra modern. Red walls made the cherry wood cabinets and the black granite with silver swirls pop.

"Can I help you with dinner?"

"No. It's fine. I have the mixed greens salad chilling in the refrigerator. Marcus is handling the steaks, baked potatoes, and mixed vegetables on the grill. I wanted a moment alone with you." Tora took a seat at the end of the table next to her.

"You did?" *What could she want? Maybe she doesn't approve of her brother with a human, instead of a shifter.*

"Raja means a lot to me. He's been all I have had for years. When our parents were killed, he raised me, protected me. Even now that I'm mated to Marcus, we're still very close. I want him happy…you seem to make him happy." She fiddled with the silverware as if nervous.

"Your brother means a lot to me."

"I don't wish to be forward, but I must ask. What are your plans? I guess the main question I want answered is once Pierce is caught, will you leave my brother behind as if he means nothing?"

Bethany's apprehension eased. Tora wanted to protect her brother. "I love Raja. I don't wish to leave him. He has been my rock through all of this. I don't know how I could have done it without him. As long as he'll have me, I'll stay by his side."

"Raja can be a hard man to live with. He cares deeply for people around him and does his best to protect everyone. He's astounding at his job of Lieutenant, but it can make it hard on his family. You would be in danger because of his position."

"First you want me with Raja, now it sounds like you're trying to scare me away from him. Which is it?" Bethany leaned into the table, trying to catch Tora's eye.

"I want you with Raja *if* you truly love him. I want you to understand what you're getting into. Raja's position can be dangerous, and he'll need a strong woman beside him; one that understands the dangers, and will take precautions when necessary. It will make his job easier if he knows his mate will be safe." Tora looked up, meeting her gaze.

"I can't honestly say I completely understand the dangers, but I'm aware of some of them. Yes, his job must be dangerous, I'll worry about him, but that's what you do when you love someone. I thought I had a quiet life with nothing to worry about, and look at me now...Pierce killed my family and has me on his hit list—that happened before I met Raja. I'll do whatever I can to aid Raja rather than distract him." She rubbed her arms trying to stifle her sudden chill. "Before coming here today, he informed me he's assigned guards for my protection. It's not something I want or feel comfortable with—yet. I know it's normal for the Lieutenant's mate to have them, but still it makes me feel awkward. Yet I didn't fight him—and I won't fight him on it. I can't protect myself against shifters. Hell, I can't protect myself against anything at the moment." She rubbed her leg as if to emphasize the point.

"We're living in a very dangerous time, everything is changing for us." Tora's nerves seemed to fall away with Bethany's answers. "Who are your guards? Have you met them yet?"

"Everyone keeps mentioning it's a dangerous time. I'm getting this feeling it's more than Pierce." She shook her head, making a mental note to ask Raja about it later. "Shadow is the Captain of the Guards. I've met her. There are four other men I have yet to meet."

Raja opened the sliding glass door and stepped in before sliding it closed behind him. "Am I interrupting?"

"Go read to your niece before she falls asleep. She's been waiting for her Uncle Raja all night."

He stepped closer to Bethany, leaning down and brushing a kiss to her ear, whispering. "You doing okay?"

Bethany nodded. His concern and affection warmed her through and through. He kissed her again and headed up the stairs.

"You two make a remarkable couple." Tora reached across the table to place her hand over Bethany's. "Welcome to the family. It's nice to finally have a sister. All Marcus gave me was another brother."

* * *

Raja enjoyed the normalcy of a family dinner. Time with his sister and her mate had been limited of late. He was grateful for the evening, happier still that Bethany enjoyed herself. Even James seemed to feel comfortable.

After the table was cleaned, leftovers stored, dishes in the dishwasher and the evening wound down, and Raja was ready to escape with his mate. He wanted to be alone with her again. Tora watched him, however, and he could sense something was on her mind. His little sister wasn't the most patient, she'd tell him before the night was over.

A light knock on the door interrupted them. "I'll get it," Raja told Tora as she served dessert and coffee in the living room.

He sensed Shadow on the other side of the door before he opened it. His mate's new Captain of the guard met his gaze quietly. "I'm sorry to bother you during your family dinner, but I need to speak with you."

Chapter Twenty-Five

"While we were training with Felix and his men…I received a message from Chris." Shadow's words incited his anger.

Raja met with Shadow and Styx in Marcus's borrowed office. He kept his voice low out of respect for his sister and her family. "The same Chris that betrayed his clan?"

"Yes. He wishes to speak with you. Connor could set up a video conference." Shadow shifted her eyes toward Styx. "I brought him with me to stay with Bethany. Chris will only be available at the number he left for a short time. This is something that would need to be done quickly."

"What does he want?"

"He only said he has some information he's sure you would want."

He stared out the window. *Chris was a good guard until his betrayal.*

"Fine. Inform Ty of the situation. Let him know I'll be there to speak with him after I find out what Chris wants. I'll need a few minutes with Tora and Bethany and then I'll meet you in the conference room."

"Styx, wait here," Raja ordered and followed Shadow out of the office.

"I'm sorry for the interruption. Something has come up. Styx is in your office; he's one of Bethany's guards. I need to deal with this now. Bethany, after you finish your dessert and wish to leave, he'll escort you back to our quarters. I hope to be back before then but if not, he'll stay with you until I'm home." He laid a hand on his mate's shoulder and squeezed gently.

"Styx?" Tora glared at him, her eyes fiery with anger. "What are you thinking?"

"He is a great warrior." Raja nodded, still rubbing Bethany's shoulder.

"He's ruthless." She roared at him. "You're trusting him with your mate...your future children."

"I know. They will be in good hands. He'll protect them at all cost."

"Who else did you assign to her guard?" Tora demanded.

"The twins Drew and Jayden, and Milo." He indulged her because they were guests in Tora's home, but it only went so far. He kissed both women on the forehead and paused to eye his sister. "I don't have time to debate this with you right now. Styx is a great warrior and I trust him to keep her safe. She's my mate—I wouldn't put her in jeopardy."

"Bethany will be staying here until you return." Tora slammed the dishrag down on the counter.

"I can make my own decisions. If this man has Raja's trust then he has mine as well." His mate threw her support to him and pride filled his chest. "Check our quarters first. I need to put my leg up. It's starting to throb a little. Go, my love. I'll be fine."

"I'll be back soon. I love you," he said, kissing her again. He turned his head toward the office. "Styx."

After the introductions, Raja slipped quietly out. He hated to leave Bethany to deal with Tora's anger over Styx as a guard, but he had little choice.

* * *

"Five minutes and I'll have you connected." Connor called out when Raja entered the conference room.

"Ty said deal with it and then swing by his quarters." Shadow handed him a printout. "Connor traced the number. That's the location. I've contacted Jinx and he has a team on the way."

"Jinx, in West Virginia, is the closest clan to Georgia?"

"It shouldn't be surprising there are no tiger clans in the south. The heat is not something most of us enjoy."

"Probably why he chose Georgia. Still no idea what Chris wants?"

Shadow shook her head.

"Raja, you're almost connected." Connor vacated the chair, allowing Raja to sit in front of the laptop.

Moments later Chris's face filled the screen. "Thank you for taking the time to speak with me, Raja."

"What is it you want, Chris?" Raja watched the screen with a lack of enthusiasm. He didn't care to be there dealing with the rogue. His betrayal cut deep through the clan.

"First I should apologize for what happened…"

"You mean for your betrayal?" The outrage was a raw wound.

"Yes, my betrayal. If I had any choice…"

"Chris, you had a choice. You chose the wrong option. Now get to the point of this call."

"I couldn't risk my sister. They had her and promised to kill her if I didn't assist them. You have a sister, so you have to understand." Chris leaned closer to the camera. "I hope the news I bring you might start building the bridge to forgiveness, that this news might take my name off your bounty list."

"What do you want in exchange for this information?" He wanted him to get to the point.

"I would ask that you call off your hunters."

"You were a worthy addition to the Alaskan Tigers before your treachery. Nevertheless, you were not worth sending a team after. If you have hunters on your trail, they're not ours. What is your information?"

"Pierce's trusted advisor, Victor, will be in San Francisco at the end of the week. He's meeting with a high-ranking Russian tiger. If anyone knows where Pierce is or what his next move is, it will be Victor."

Raja sat in the chair unmoving while he ran through the facts he knew of Victor, which were few. He nodded and turned off the communication.

"Find out everything you can about Victor, report to me the minute you find anything interesting. If I don't hear from you, we'll have a conference at ten o'clock tomorrow morning," he directed Connor, his thumb and forefinger rubbing the arch of his nose. "This could all be a setup."

Raja rose and glanced at Shadow. "Get back to your evening off. They might be few and far between if things continue on this path. I'll speak with Ty and then I'll find Bethany, and we'll be retiring for the night. You won't be needed unless something happens."

"Thank you." She nodded, following him out of the conference room. She made the left, as he turned right toward Ty's quarters.

* * *

"Ahh Raja please sit. Can I get you anything to drink? Coffee perhaps?"

"Thank you, Tabitha, but no. I need a moment of Ty's time please." Raja yawned. His eyes felt grainy from lack of sleep.

"He'll be right out. He's meeting with Felix in his office."

Tabitha curled up on the large black sofa, propping herself up with red throw pillows. A romance novel carefully laid aside to keep the page. All around the room, small, feminine changes added to the warmth of Ty's formerly masculine quarters. The red throw pillows, new curtains with brighter prints, everything brought a female touch.

"Sorry to keep you waiting. Felix and I were going over the changes in the guard schedules now that you have taken Drew and Jayden from the grounds guards, not to mention Styx and Milo." Ty stepped out of his office followed by Felix.

"If it is inconvenient, I can make other arrangements."

"No, it's fine. We have promoted two boys from the training class for grounds duty and will be testing some of the guards to move into the positions Milo and Styx left. Keeping Bethany safe is priority as well. Now, what did Chris contact you for?"

"Victor will be in San Francisco at the end of the week." Raja leaned forward, his elbows resting on his knees.

"It could be a setup."

"I thought of that as well. But he asked for us to remove the hunters we had on him."

"We didn't send hunters after him." Ty took as seat next to his mate, pulling her feet into his lap.

"I'm aware of that. I believe they're Pierce's. Once you've betrayed someone, it would be hard to trust them. If he has any sense, he would realize the need to exterminate him. I have Connor working on finding out everything on Victor." Raja rubbed the arch of his nose. "Chris honestly believed the hunters were ours, and doesn't seem to suspect Pierce. He exchanged the information for the safety of himself and his sister. He hasn't changed—he's selfish. He only contacted us to get the hunters off his ass. He's still probably thinking if the information is correct then we'll take the hunters off him."

"Even if the information is good I want him taken out. He's too dangerous to keep alive. He betrayed us once; he'll do it again if the chance is given. Our mates are much too valuable to risk it." Ty rubbed his hand over Tabitha's leg.

Raja nodded. "I told Connor to be at the conference room at ten o'clock, just key people for this meeting. Chris still has friends among the clan. I doubt anyone else will betray us. But I don't want to give them the opportunity. Felix, Marcus, Thomas, Adam, Connor, Shadow, Styx, and us and our mates."

Ty nodded. "Let Lance and Spencer know they're on standby until further notice. I want them ready to leave at a moment's notice. They'll be the ones we send to deal with Chris."

Marissa Dobson

Chapter Twenty-Six

Raja found Styx standing inside the door, looking uncomfortable and on guard, when he returned to his quarters.

"While here you may make yourself at home, as long as you are ready to spring to action if the situation calls for it. You don't have to stand by the door at all times," Raja said, closing the door behind him.

"That's what I told him." Bethany sat on the couch, her knee propped up on pillows.

"Styx, thank you for bringing her back. I hope my sister didn't give you too much trouble."

The guard's quick, negative headshake was met with Bethany's laughter, lightening the mood throughout the room.

"Don't lie to him." Bethany grinned. "Tora's very special and I like her, but she has a stubborn streak. It wasn't until Marcus stepped in that she backed down."

"Then I apologize for her actions. Tora has heard rumors from the battlefield. It has left her a little cautious." He shook his head, amused and exasperated. At least his headstrong sister listened to her mate. "Marcus is a smart man. He knows better than to question my decisions. Tora, however, likes to press her luck. You think she's bad now, but she was quite the handful before she mated. She's always been one to speak her mind and didn't care how much trouble that got her in."

"I'll understand if you wish to override Shadow's decision for me as Bethany's guard." Styx offered, but the look in his eyes said he wanted to remain her guard.

"No. I trust you to keep Bethany safe."

"Very well." He stepped away. "If that is all I'll retired to my cabin."

"Be at the conference room at ten tomorrow morning," Raja dismissed him.

"Very well. If you need me, I'll keep my ear piece in." Styx slipped out the door, leaving them alone. Raja secured it and went to his mate. His duty handled, his desire to be with her overrode all else.

"What happened?"

"Into bed." He lifted her from the couch as if she weighed nothing. She wrapped her arms around his neck, snuggling her head into his chest.

"You're tired. I can walk."

"I know you can, but I want to feel you against me." He nudged the door open with his foot, laid her on the bed and slipped off his shoes and his gun holster before crawling in next to her.

"You're still dressed." She rolled to cuddle into his body.

"I don't care. Undress later." His eyes fluttered as his head hit the pillow. "Chris contacted us tonight. I had to take care of it."

"Who's Chris?"

"He...betrayed..." He wanted to answer her questions, but holding her and knowing she was safe let him relax and he tumbled headlong into sleep.

* * *

Curiosity nibbled at Bethany and, when she caught sight of his phone still clipped to his pants. She retrieved it and found Ty's cell number and texted him, hoping Tabitha was still awake. *Tabitha, it's Bethany. Who's Chris? Raja fell asleep before I got the whole story.*

Moments later the cell phone vibrated in her hand. *He betrayed us to Pierce. Tried to trade me for his sister.*

Sick to her stomach, Bethany stared at the cell and waited what seemed like ages, when it vibrated again. *Said he has info about a member of Pierce's gang. Geek Connor is on it. We'll know more tomorrow. Sleep. You both need it.*

* * *

"What's this?" Raja woke Bethany sometime in the middle of the night. Her hand still clenched the cell phone.

"Umm."

"Who did you call?"

"No one." She dropped the phone to the comforter as if it burned her.

"You're not a prisoner here, Bethany. If you want to call someone, you can as long as you're careful not to give our location away." He grabbed the phone before rolling over to place it on the nightstand.

"I didn't call anyone. I texted Tabitha." She pulled her bottom lip between her teeth, biting it.

"Tabitha doesn't have a cell phone. We ordered a new untraceable cell for her, but it hasn't arrived yet. Our cells are custom-ordered to make them harder to trace. Which reminds me that I'll have to order you one as well."

"Ty's cell phone. Check if you don't believe me."

"I believe you." He put his hand on her waist, pulling her closer to him. "Why?"

"You fell asleep on me. I couldn't sleep not knowing who this Chris was."

Raja laughed, a rich laugh that gently caressed her skin. "Sorry. I was exhausted. I didn't mean to fall asleep on you. Did they answer your questions?"

"Somewhat. He deceived the clan."

He nodded, kissing her neck. "He gave me information on Victor, Pierce's trusted advisor. We have a team ready to move if the information checks out. Connor's working on it. There's a briefing at ten you're more than welcome to attend."

"The plane…"

"Oh, that's right, your parents' and sister's bodies will arrive for the services today. We'll find out what time. I'll reschedule the briefing if I have to, I'll be there with you."

A lump rose in her throat as her loss struck home again. She swallowed hard, and took a deep breath. "Uncle James will be there, and this is important…the briefing." She ran her hand over his chest, playing with his soft black chest hair.

"I'll be there." He kissed her forehead. "I love you, Bethany."

"I love you too. Are you still tired?"

"Why?" He played with a loose strand of her hair.

"I want to feel your hands on my body. I want to feel you in me."

He smiled. "Come here."

Chapter Twenty-Seven

Raja and Ty stood at the end of the conference table, their mates seated at their respective sides. Felix sat next to Tabitha and Shadow next to Bethany, giving the clear picture of the hierarchy. Marcus, Thomas, Adam, Connor and Styx took the remaining chairs.

"Connor, what did you find?" Raja took a sip of coffee.

"It would seem the information is correct. Victor is flying out of Dulles International Airport in Virginia on Friday and has booked a hotel room close to the airport in San Francisco through the weekend."

"Careless for him to book in his name." Ty watched the information scroll on screen in front of him.

"He's cocky. He probably didn't believe he would be caught, that no one would be able to track him or want to track him." Connor hit a button, and a picture replaced the flight and hotel information. "This is his most current picture. Taken less than a year ago."

The man on the screen before them looked to be in his late fifties. His dark salt and pepper hair was more white than dark, and gave him a weathered look. His dark, soulless eyes stared elsewhere. People were a pawn in his game.

"How can a man this old be so naïve? He has to suspect you could be monitoring travel arrangements made in the names of anyone associated with Pierce." Bethany eyed the board with disgust.

"Maybe he's encouraging us to try to take him down." Tabitha leaned forward in her chair, angling herself to get a better view of the man. "I know him."

"You know him? How?" Ty touched his mate's shoulder.

"He came into the restaurant where I worked at in Pittsburgh, I waited on him. He was there the day I came home and discovered Ty's letter attached to my door. Two days before Pierce turned up at my apartment."

"Did he say anything?"

"He mentioned he was in town to reacquaint with an old friend…" She looked at Ty with glossy tears in her eyes. "You don't think…he meant me, do you?"

The room pulsed with Ty's rage. Raja understood the fear and the fury. If Ty had been a little later finding Tabitha, she could have been at the mercy of Pierce and his gang.

"I won't lie to you, Tabitha, it's very likely he meant you. You're safe here. We'll bring him down." Raja turned to Conner. "What else do you know about him? Does he have any family? A mate? Children?"

"No family on record. Parents are deceased. He's a born shifter and joined forces with Pierce shortly after Pierce's change. His beliefs are different from Pierce's. He wants to rid the world of the lesser shifters and believes the mate, or mates in his version, are only there for breeding."

"Mates?"

"According to what I have found about him, he believes we have multiple mates. Our first true mate will lead us to our other mates."

"Interesting. Especially since he's unmated. One would think he would put his beliefs into action." Raja glanced at the clock on the wall. *Forty minutes until the plane lands.* "He'll be there in two days. We'll send two teams, along with other men from Jinx's clan in West Virginia, to take him down and if possible brought back alive to a secure location."

"Lance and Spencer are standing by to leave. Leo, if you would go pack your stuff and join them, you will be part of the second team. Adam, we would like for you to head the team, reporting directly to Raja." Ty rubbed his mate's shoulder as he watched the young guard with interest.

"Yes, sir. I'm honored. Thank you." Adam rose to follow Leo out.

"You've earned it. Give us another few minutes of your time and then you can pack and brief the team before the plane leaves."

Adam nodded, returning to his seat. The door closed behind Leo.

"Adam, it's doubtful Pierce will be there but if he is, we'll send more soldiers. Do your best to find out his reason for meeting with the Russian tiger. Confiscate whatever evidence that might be in his room, anything that might assist us. Lastly, if possible, take him alive. We'll want to interrogate him. If he has others with him, do whatever you deem necessary. Jinx's men will be leaving late this evening and will meet you there. I'll be available at any time, and we'll have more men standing by." Raja poured himself another cup of coffee. He needed all the caffeine he could get. Their long days were going to get longer. "Unless you have any questions, you're dismissed."

"Thank you. I won't let you down." Adam stood quickly, leaving the room in a hurry.

"Now the rest of you, once Victor is taken down, or he's aware there are men on him, it could lead to an attack on the compound. I want everyone on a code red until you hear otherwise from Ty or me. There need to be two guards on Tabitha and Bethany round the clock." He caught the twin dirty looks the females favored him with, but he was glad they didn't voice their displeasure. "When in their quarters with their mates, guards are to be outside the main door, or may be dismissed for the night but on call. Felix and Shadow will assign shifts for each mate. That will be all for now. Shadow, Styx, if you two could wait outside while Ty, our mates and I have a word, then we can meet the plane."

"Felix, if you'll wait with them."

The guards filed out of the conference room, leaving the air heavy with tension. Raja knew it was only a matter of moments before the women let loose their displeasure over the guards. Who would be first...his bet was on Tabitha. Bethany would wait until later when they were alone and she could wrap him around her finger.

"Round-the-clock guards? Is that really necessary?" Unhappiness soured Tabitha's voice.

"Yes, Tabby, it is. You're my mate, and I want you safe. If something comes up and either of us is called away, we want to know our mates will be safe. If the situation calls for it, you'll be guarded together. Four guards are better than two. I don't want to hear any arguing from either of you. Tabitha, you have been here when there was an attack on the compound. Bethany, you know what Pierce is capable of. Don't fight us on this—neither of you will win." Ty had less patience for the argument than Raja did.

The protest in Tabitha extinguished and she nodded.

"If you believe it's necessary," Bethany agreed.

"I do." Raja laid a hand over hers. "The plane will be landing shortly. We should..."

Bethany nodded.

Before she could stand, Tabitha spoke. "If you don't mind, Ty and I would like to accompany you. Tora has arranged the memorial service for this evening."

"Thank you." Tears glistened in Bethany's eyes, and Raja could feel his mate's gratitude. He saw the spark in her that wasn't there before, as if she'd found a place within their close-knit group.

Marissa Dobson

Chapter Twenty-Eight

The number of clan members standing at the landing strip overwhelmed Raja. Standing front and center were Tora and her mate Marcus.

It looks as though all the clan members are here.

Tears streamed down Bethany's face and her lips trembled.

"We wanted to be here to support you." Tora reached out and touched Bethany's arm.

"Thank you, Tora." Raja wrapped his arm around Bethany, drawing her as close to him as her crutches would allow. *Maybe I didn't do too bad raising that big-mouthed sister of mine. She's turned out to be an amazing woman.*

"Yes, thank you." Bethany cried in a tearful voice.

"Your face will freeze if you keep crying." Tora smiled sadly, and wiped Bethany's cheeks with a tissue. "Sorry...I guess it's the mother in me. Come on, Doc requested a chair for you. He doesn't want you to overdo it on the knee."

Walking through the crowd, he realized there were only a few members not present. *Only the guards on duty are missing.*

As if Tora read his mind, she spoke. "After learning of the memorial service everyone wanted to show their support. The guards on duty send their sympathies but were unable to get away."

"Where's Scarlet?" Raja gave Tora's hand a squeeze, letting her know how thankful he was for all she did.

"She's with Daniella. It's much too cold for her to be out here."

Tora had gone all out, a tent waited with chairs and a bench up front. A table filled with thermoses of warm liquids and if he knew his sister, at least one of them had his special, dark roasted coffee waiting for him.

She directed them to the large bench. "Sit. I'll get you something warm to drink."

Raja sat with Bethany to his left, followed by Tabitha, Ty and Felix. Shadow and Styx sat on Bethany's right. When she rested her head gently on Raja's shoulder, he wrapped his arms around her.

"Your sister is incredible," she whispered.

"Don't tell her that. It will make things unbearable for Marcus. She already believes he couldn't get along without her, not even for a day." His lips curved into a smile.

"I distinctly remember someone saying men need their mates. We complete them."

"You can't use my own words against me," he teased.

Tora returned with a tray of coffees and hot cocoa for Raja, Bethany, Tabitha, Ty and the guards. "This one's your special blend." She pointed to the cup closest to Raja. "Bethany, I think you might enjoy the hot cocoa. It's unlike anything you ever tasted before."

"Bethany, you must try it. It is amazing." Tabitha grabbed one of the hot cocoa cups off the tray, her face glowing with pleasure.

"Okay." She took one of the cups, breathing in the aroma. "It smells delicious."

"Taste it," Tabitha encouraged.

She took a small sip and moaned. "Oh my!"

"I told you. Delicious. The kitchen staff makes it with real chocolate, none of that powdered stuff." Tabitha wrapped her hands around the mug, and sipped.

A distant sound of a plane engine sobered the mood. Raja knew even after hearing from the detective, the arrangements were made and so on, Bethany still held on to a glimmer of hope that it was all a bad dream. That was all about to come crashing down around them when the coffins were unloaded, and he could do nothing to ease her grief.

Please let my love and support be enough to get her through this difficult time.

The plane came into view and Bethany trembled.

"I'm here, love."

"I'm fine." She tried to put on a brave face, but Raja saw through it.

Marcus and Tora took a seat on the other side of Styx, when someone laid a hand on Bethany's shoulder, brushing his arm that was around her in the process. Raja growled, ready to take the head off whoever touched his mate. He turned to find James.

"Sorry, it's been so long since I've been around other shifters, let alone a mated pair." James pulled his hand away as if Raja burned it.

"Uncle James, I'm glad you're here." Bethany turned slightly to see him. "We're having a service for Mom, Dad and Jamie this evening."

"I'll be there." He stood behind them as the plane landed.

A man in cowboy boots and hat stepped out of the plane and walked directly toward them. *Must be Jinx's man who accompanied them.*

"Bethany, Raja, I'm Jinx the Alpha of the West Virginia clan. I have brought your family home." He bowed his head, radiating sympathy.

"Thank you." Tears flooded down her checks.

"Welcome to Alaska." Ty stood, shaking his hand. "Thank you for bringing our clan member's family home."

"I'd like to ask for assistance with the caskets. We can place them where you would like, and then Bethany can have the time she needs. There's no need to do it out here in the cold." Jinx spoke to Ty but his gaze, full of sympathy, was on Bethany.

"Styx, Marcus, would you please gather other men and help him?" Raja rubbed his hand down her arm. They nodded and rose. "We'll show you to the area once you have unloaded them."

Ty stood. "On behalf of Bethany and Raja, I'd like to thank everyone for joining us. We appreciate the support for Bethany. We'll have the memorial service this evening and would be pleased if you join us."

No one moved as the caskets were carried off. Ty, Tabitha and Felix led the men to the ballroom. It was the only room capable of accommodating the large service and it was, already decorated with flowers and a large picture of Bethany with her family in the center where the coffins would go. Bethany and Raja, along with Shadow and James, followed with Tora behind, giving them privacy.

"Oh my." Bethany stopped as she saw the picture.

"Jinx sent us the picture. I asked Tora to have a larger one made and hung here. It seemed appropriate."

"It's wonderful. Thank you, Raja."

Jinx came to them, carrying an urn. "Bethany, I'm assuming Raja explained to you that due to the condition of your sister, she had to be cremated immediately."

Bethany nodded, running her hand over the urn.

"If you'd place her on the small table between her parents, that will be fine." Raja nodded toward the table in question.

"I want to see my parents." Bethany looked from Jinx to Raja. "Please."

"I don't know if that is a good idea, love."

"I have to. I need to see, to know that this is real."

"They did the best they could, but still it is an unpleasant sight," Jinx warned before turning to place the urn on the table.

"I wish you wouldn't, but if it's what you want, then okay." Raja wanted to wrap his arms around her, but those dang crutches were in the way. Instead he rested his hand on the small of her back.

"I want to do it alone. Just us. No one else needs to remember my family like this. When they think of them, I want them to see the picture you hung."

"James?" He queried quietly.

She shook her head.

"Okay, I'll need a few minutes to clear the room. Why don't you sit down while I do it?"

* * *

Bethany couldn't get the image of her parents in their caskets out of her mind. She sat curled on the couch, the cup of tea Raja made her untouched in her hand, staring into space. *The undertaker did the best he could, but you could still see they met a brutal end.*

"I want him to feel the same agony he put my family through. I want him to beg for mercy, plead for his life to be spared."

"You're angry now, but I promised you we'll find Pierce. When we do, your parents and Jamie as well as Tabitha's parents, will get the justice they deserve. He has blood on his hands, and it's only a matter of time before we catch him. With any luck Victor could be a vital key to Pierce's location." Raja squatted before her, taking her chin between his fingers to make her look at him. "I need you to be strong. I'll see he gets what's owed to him."

"No." Horror shook her out of her thoughts. "You can't."

"Shh, love. You're shaking like a leaf."

"Please, don't. He could kill you. I can't bear to lose you too. Please, Raja." Terror ricocheted through her.

"Bethany, nothing is going to happen to me. I promise you. A bitten tiger couldn't take me down. His strength is nothing compared to mine. I'm not going anywhere. You're stuck with me for the long haul." Raja's hand went to his ear. "We'll be here," he said, hitting the button on his ear bud.

"What's going on?"

"Ty and Tabitha are on their way. I should put more coffee on." He rose, still holding her hand. "I promise you everything will be fine. All you have to do it trust me." He seemed convinced that everything would be fine, but still in the back of her mind worries lingered.

Marissa Dobson

Chapter Twenty-Nine

"I'm sorry to intrude today of all days." Tabitha sat next to Ty on the loveseat; she'd brought the book her father passed down to her. In the letter her father left her, along with the book, he promised that everything she needed to know could be found within its pages. It had been passed down in her family from generation to generation, each adding their own information, but it also contained a secret section that only unlocked with her touch. It was her guide to uniting all tiger shifters.

"Tabitha, we're family, it's not intrusion. Something is bothering you. What is it?"

"Raja, have you explained this to Bethany?" Tabitha ran her hand over the book.

He nodded. "Shadow as well. Being the Captain of Bethany's Guards, she needed to know what trouble could lay ahead." He cuddled Bethany against him. His mate had taken emotional blow after emotional blow, but she bore up with remarkable strength. She was more than the right match for him.

"After we separated earlier, we took Jinx to his brother, Lukas's cabin. Jinx is going to stay on at least through the weekend, depending on what happens in San Francisco. When we returned, I felt as if the book called to me, the magic caressed my skin, drawing me to it, impossible to deny. I went to it and found this." She unlocked the book, letting it fall open to where she bookmarked it, before handing it to Raja.

Now that you have gone through the change and your team is assembled, it's time to begin uniting the tigers. Having your Lieutenant, Raja mated makes for a stronger core, and Bethany might be unaware yet but she'll play a key role throughout the transition as well. Expect a new tiger named Galen soon. He's a healer, he knows nothing of this situation, and means you no harm. He has come to heal Bethany.

Danger surrounds you not only with your battle against Pierce but also with your tasks ahead. You'll need your core group and warriors at their full strength, uninjured. Galen will see to your injuries and keep you at your strongest.

Felix, Marcus and Thomas are wonderful choices as your Enforcers. Shadow is also an unexpected yet valued addition. She'll be most helpful in the coming months. Styx will also be a treasured addition as a warrior, as well as a guard. You have chosen well.

The first step lies with Jinx. He needs to be brought into your trusted confidence, and you need to form a bond between the West Virginian and Alaskan clans. Family has run the West Virginia clan for generations. That doesn't mean they aren't the strongest, because Jinx would put the other members of his clan to shame if he showed his full power.

This will help to put fears to rest before they reveal themselves. Once the tigers are united, they will remain as they are with an Alpha and Lieutenant to each clan. However, instead of running things their way and reporting to no one, they will report to you. Look at it as if the ten of you are the Committee of Tigers. Tabitha and Ty being the Queen and King, having the final say. This will calm some of the disputes that could arise if shifters were losing their positions of power.

There's a young woman, Robin Zimmer. She's human, innocent, but became a pawn in a debt her ex-husband owed to Pierce. Trading Robin for his own life got him nowhere, as he's dead and Robin is on the run. Find Robin. She holds key information about Pierce and his members.

When Raja and Bethany finished reading it, he handed the book to Shadow, who sat cross-legged in the chair angled between the couch and loveseat. Felix sat beside her on a chair he brought from the kitchen.

"Have you put Connor on finding this Robin Zimmer?" Raja asked.

"Not yet. This was our first stop. Connor's still working on digging up any information on Victor and the Russian tiger." Ty shook his head.

"Zimmer...Bobby Zimmer? No..." Bethany whispered.

"What?" Raja asked at his mate's mumbles.

"In high school I knew a Robert 'Bobby' Zimmer. He married a girl, but I thought her name was Rose. It could have been Robin. We weren't really friends, more like distant acquaintances. I remember

Mom telling me he died a few months ago. But it couldn't be the same Bobby, could it?"

"It's a good lead. I'll have Connor start there, and we'll see if we turn anything up," Ty said, taking his arm from around his mate to lean forward. "I know it's bad timing, but I'd like to meet with Jinx today. It's something I don't want to put off any longer. Raja, I'd like you by my side, but Bethany, I understand and am sure Jinx will as well if you wish to rest."

Before Raja could speak, Bethany did. "We'll be there. When?"

"If you're okay with the decision, I'll send for Jinx now. I'd say it's best to get it over with quickly. After the service this evening, I'm sure you'll want to be alone." Ty cocked his head slightly toward Felix. "Would you see if Jinx is available to join us?"

"Very well." Felix rose.

"I'll bring in a kitchen chair." Shadow unfolded her small frame from the chair and stood.

"What do you think the book meant when it said I'll play a key role through the transition? I'm merely human—how could I be of great assistance?"

"Only time will tell, but if it's in the book you can count on it. As for your merely human comment, you couldn't stand against Pierce and his gang in hand-to-hand combat, but there are still things you can do. Once your knee is healed, Raja will work with you, training you to defend yourself if the case calls for it. As well as weapons training. We won't have you unable to protect yourself. I hope that you'll never need the skills he gives you, but it's better to have them and not need them. We have assigned you guards not because you're human, but because you're Raja's mate. You and Tabitha are the Alpha women of the clan—you're to be protected at all costs. The guards will be there to protect you if we cannot be."

* * *

Jinx strode into the room, pulled his cowboy hat off and ran his hand through his dark hair. Felix followed behind him.

"Jinx, thank you for joining us. Please have a seat." Ty welcomed him.

"My pleasure. What can I do for you?" Jinx took the chair that Shadow vacated earlier.

"Do you know the legends of a Queen of the Tigers?" Raja dove right into the reason for the meeting.

"Doesn't everyone?" Jinx shook his head.

"Tabitha is the Queen of the Tigers. She comes from the line of tigers, and her father passed down this book to her. It explains everything and will walk her through the trials and tribulations of uniting the tiger shifters." Ty ran his hand over his mate's leg.

"How do you expect to unite us?"

"It will take time, there will be many steps. According to the book we need to form a bond with you, and unite the West Virginian and Alaskan tigers." Tabitha held open the book to the most recent page and handed it to Jinx. "We found this in the book today, after we left Lukas's cabin."

"I always hoped that I would live to see the day we would be united. I never thought I would have anything to do with the process, let alone hold this book in my hands." Jinx looked down at the book in astonishment. "Anything you need from me you shall have. My clan is small, there are only fifteen of us, but we're at your disposal. Does your clan know she's the Queen?"

"Not completely. Some suspect it but things have been nonstop since Tabitha arrived. First, the homecoming ball, then the videos from Pierce, finding Bethany, her family murder... There hasn't been time to explain things to them. There are approximately ten who do know—the ones in this room as well as Connor, Marcus, Tora and Thomas. We'll be briefing Styx today as well. The Alaskan clan will be briefed soon, with any luck before you return to West Virginia, but when would depend on how the Victor situation turned out." Ty ran his hand down his mate's leg. "Once the clan is told it will still need to remain quiet until we're ready to start the process of uniting all tigers. When you return to your people, you can give them the information as well, as long as they keep it amongst themselves."

"Understood. Lukas is my best warrior. You could say he's my unofficial head of security. He is powerful enough to be my Lieutenant but prefers being in the field. We were discussing your issues with Pierce, and he's interested in being in the front lines of this war. He planned to approach the subject with you, but needed to seek my approval first. He has my consent. If you would be interested in his skills, he can stay here among your clan. I believe he would be of great service to you." Jinx handed the book back to Tabitha.

"He's more than welcome to stay as long as he understands the hierarchy here. He's young and would need to work his way up. Prove his worth, per say. He seems to fit well with the other guards and clan members. Raja?" Ty opened the floor for Raja to share his thoughts.

"I agree. Lukas is young. He'll need to prove himself not only to us, but also to the guards and members. Due to his injuries, I haven't seen his fighting skills yet. We need someone to start training some of the younger clan members. With his age he might be perfect for the position."

Raja's ear bud sprang to life. *There's a tiger out here asking for you, Raja.*

He sent Ty a look to let him know something was happening before slipping out from under Bethany. "Excuse me," he said to the room, moving toward the window. He hit the button on his ear communication to allow the guard station to hear him. "What's his name?"

He could see the main gate, the guards gathered there blocking the entrance, but he couldn't make out what or whom they were keeping out.

"Says his name is Galen. He has some crazy story about a dream telling him to come here and ask for you. He seems nervous."

Raja recognized Korbin's voice. He was one of the regular border patrol guards. "I'm sending Shadow. If she believes his story, escort him back with her."

He turned the button again to end the communication with the gatehouse and turned to find all eyes on him. "Galen's here. Shadow, as a precaution go and listen to his story. If you believe him, bring him back."

Shadow nodded and stood, slipping away without a word.

"Ty, Tabitha, I think it would be best if you weren't here. I know the book says he brings us no harm, but let's play this safe." Raja looked back out the window to see if Shadow arrived yet.

"I disagree," Tabitha said when Ty stood. "If Galen's a healer, we need him. Maybe we could convince him we need him here. If we're going to war with Pierce, having a healer handy could mean the life or death of one of our members."

"She's right." Bethany twisted and looked at him. She'd disagreed so little with his decisions, he knew it was right to listen to her on this.

"Felix, get Marcus and Styx in here. If you're going to stay I want more guards here now." Raja flexed his hands. "I still think you two should be somewhere safer. If things go ape shit..."

"Things will be fine," Tabitha reassured Raja.

"Now you see what I go through. She's stubborn." Ty laughed. "I'd say they're going to keep us on our toes."

The men laughed and it brought them a brief respite from the tension. But events were proceeding swiftly. Raja glanced back out the window, and watched Shadow approach their newcomer.

Too swiftly.

Chapter Thirty

"My Queen." Galen turned out to be an old man in his seventies. He dropped to his knees mere steps inside the door, his head low. "All my life I've waited for you. I knew one day I'd find you. I tried not to let my devotion waiver, but it was hard at times. People doubt the legends, but I knew the truth."

"How do you know?" Raja asked, inserting himself between the old man and Ty and Tabitha. The couple rose when Galen dropped to his knees. Despite the book's promises, Raja wanted to be close enough to take him out before he had a chance to do any harm.

"I had a dream when I was a child about the Tiger Queen who would someday be in need of my service. I've traveled, hoping to find her. Two days ago I had another dream that pressed on me to come here." He looked up and focused on Tabitha. "My Queen, I'm at your service. Anything I can do for you. I've been waiting all my life to be in your presence."

"Galen, is it true you can heal with your touch?" Tabitha asked, circling around Raja to stand at his side.

"Yes, my Queen."

"Please call me Tabitha. Besides the people in this room no one else is aware I'm the Queen the legends speak of." When Galen nodded, she continued, "If it's true, heal Raja's mate, Bethany."

Watching Galen reach toward his injured mate, Raja couldn't swallow the growl in his throat.

"I mean her no harm. In order to heal I must place my hands on her. Come hold your mate. Her injuries are extensive, and this may cause some discomfort."

Raja took the place behind Bethany, wrapped his arms around her and pressed his lips to her temple. "You okay with this?" He whispered in her ear.

"Let's get it over with." She nodded.

"If you could come stand by her as well? You might need to hold her still if she bucks." Galen asked Ty as he slipped off his gloves.

"You said there would be discomfort. I can handle it. Why would I need Ty to hold me down as well?" Bethany asked, worry coating the words.

"It depends on the injury and the person's pain threshold. Your knee is seriously injured. Without my healing it's possible you'll always have a limp after a long recovery period. I won't lie—this could be more painful than just some discomfort, but it will get you back up on your feet today. It's your choice, ma'am." Galen kneeled next to the couch.

"It's your choice, love. If you don't want to do this, you don't have to." Raja held her close. The thought of his mate being in pain at Galen's hands made him want to tear Galen's head off.

"Do it. Better to be whole all at once than worry about the future. I can take it." Bethany clenched her jaw.

"Very well. Whatever happens, Raja, do not take your hands off her. Maintain skin-to-skin contact. A mate's touch will help the pain be more bearable." Galen undid the air cast, sliding the pant leg up. "I have to have skin contact." His voice remained patient, seemingly understanding Raja's objections.

Control yourself. Raja scolded himself, trying to rein in his basic instincts. His muscles constricted with tension, his claws threaten to spring forth. "Let's get this done."

"Everyone ready?" Galen asked, his hands hovering inches from her knee.

As his hands made contact with her leg, a warm, golden aura formed around her knee. Bethany screeched with pain, struggling under Raja's grasp. He held tight to her, trying to take her pain. "It's almost over, love."

I can't stand seeing her in this kind of pain. She's my mate and I couldn't stop her injury. Now she's suffering more for me. When he didn't think he could take any more, his heart breaking from the pain his mate suffered, it ended as quickly as it began. Bethany collapsed against him, softly moaning.

Galen bent back on his heels, shaking his head. "It can't be," he said repeatedly.

"What can't be?" Raja asked, still soothing his mate.

"She's human." Galen said still not making any sense.

"What are you mumbling about?"

"Her body fought me."

"So? You told us that would happen. What are you going on about? Is she not healed?" His frustration peaked. *If she went through all that pain and isn't healed, I'm going to hurt someone.*

"That's different. Normally they show signs of pain, fighting to get away, struggling and hollering. They don't normally fight the healing. She did." Galen slipped his gloves back into place, still watching Bethany closely.

"What does that mean?" Tabitha asked, coming to stand next to her mate by the couch.

"It shouldn't be possible, since she is human...but she's a healer."

"Then wouldn't she heal herself?" Raja held Bethany close, could feel her fatigue as if it were his own.

"Most would. Except she hasn't accepted her gift." Galen rose from the floor, moving back to his chair. "Bethany, have you ever noticed anything different about yourself?"

She shook her head, eyes closed.

"Have your injuries ever healed quicker?"

Realization filled Raja. "He tried to strangle her. There were marks on her from where his fingers dug into her, and there were bruises as well. They're gone. I never realized it before."

"It proves my point. Bethany, you're a healer. I can work with you, teach you the skill."

"But I'm human." The exhaustion she felt echoed in her voice.

"You must have shifters in your family somewhere or you wouldn't have the gift." Galen looked down at her for confirmation, but it never came. "She needs her rest. Whenever she's ready I'll work with her. It shouldn't take long for her to develop the skills, as she's already beginning the process on her body without her knowledge."

"Galen, we would like for you to stay with us if you have no other commitments. The future is dangerous, and to have a healer here would be beneficial." Tabitha looked down at Bethany. "Well two healers. We can provide you with a guest cabin if you would stay."

"Thank you. As I told you before, I'm at your service. I'll stay as long as I'm needed."

"Very well. Felix, could you have one of the guards show Galen to a guest cabin?" Ty looked to another guard, who still stood near the door. "Korbin, we'd like to speak with you in our quarters about what you heard here. Raja, we'll be back in thirty minutes for the memorial service, and we can all go together."

Marissa Dobson

Chapter Thirty-One

Bethany curled up beside him, and they watched the aurora borealis lights through the large floor to ceiling windows.

"It wasn't all a dream—I'm really a healer?" Bethany's head rested on his shoulder.

"It would seem so. Galen has offered to work with you to bring your ability out, if you're willing."

"I want to learn. It will be a great asset for your people."

"For our people. You're a leader of this clan too." He stroked his fingers through her hair, soothing himself with her nearness. "You should get some rest. Galen said you would be tired from all that your body went through during the healing, not including the stress of everything else."

"Soon." She stared out the window. Something weighed on her mind, but Raja didn't want to press her after all she had been through.

"Bethany." Using his finger he gently guided her head so she could look at him. "Are you okay?"

She gave him a halfhearted smile. "If I…"

"What love?"

"If I had been there…maybe…I could have healed them."

He was painfully aware she meant her family. "He would have killed you as well."

"If I could have…"

"Say you came in after it happened, after he was gone…there still would have been nothing you could have done. You didn't even know you had this ability. Without training you wouldn't have been able to call it forth and heal them." He ran his thumb over the dimple in her chin. "Bethany, listen to me. There's nothing you could have done to change this outcome. If you were there, it would have meant one more life lost at Pierce's hands."

She sat silent for a few minutes as if she processed what he said. "The memorial service was beautiful. Now that I'm back on my feet, could we have Tora and Marcus to dinner to thank them? I'll cook…tomorrow if you could arrange it. She put together a wonderful service for people she didn't even know."

"I'll call her in the morning if you're still up for it." He kissed the top of her head.

I can never repay Tora for putting it together. It gave Bethany the peace she needed. The appreciation in her eyes—the look in them now is more than I could have hoped for.

"Bethany, there's a place on the edge of our compound lot. It's a small sitting area, beautiful views…my parents are buried there. I thought after the ashes of your parents came back we could bury them there with your sister."

"I would like that." She looked up at him. "I love you, Raja." She kissed him.

She kissed him with fervor and his passion roused. She slipped on top of him, straddling his lap. She pushed her fingers through his hair and tugged the leather strap he used to tie it back with free. "I love your hair when it's loose. I want to run my hands through it while you're inside me. I need you now."

He slid his hands under the loose nightshirt, delighted to find her naked beneath.

"Surprise, surprise," she whispered softly against his ear. She grazed his earlobe with her teeth; the lightest of tugs and then traced a path of kisses down his neck.

"It would appear someone planned to seduce me," he teased, and helped pull her shirt over her head. Her dusty pink nipples called to him, and he indulged himself. Drawing one into his mouth and laving the tip with his tongue. Her back arched and she clung to him, nails digging into his shoulders.

She slipped a hand between them to unbutton his jeans and the zipper glided downwards loudly. He sighed in anticipation, grazing the pebbled tip of her nipple with his teeth.

"I want you in me." She stroked his shaft, a gentle demand in the caress of her warm hands.

"Someone is impatient tonight." He rubbed his head in the crook of her shoulder, marking her. *You're mine. You'll always be mine.*

"You have been so cautious with me, with my injured knee. Tonight I want all of you. I don't want you to hold back."

He kept his mouth shut. He wanted to tell her that he would always have to hold back to a degree. Without a tight leash, his strength could hurt her, but he angled between her thighs and eased inside, the slow friction a delicious torture for them both.

As his shaft slid firmly into her, he paused to let them both regain their breath, before he placed his hands on her hips and helped them find the rhythm they needed. She writhed against him, encouraging him with sweet little gasps and tight muscles. Every stroke added to the tension coiling at the base of his spine. Bracing one hand against the bed, he slid the other between them and teased the tight bundle of nerves.

Her body clenched around him and she clawed at his back, marking him. The simple act reached his soul and he purred as she exploded around him. The heat lacing his spine turned molten and his climax followed seconds later. Throwing his head back, he roared.

They collapsed together, and he rolled so she sprawled across his chest. "I love you, Bethany."

He reveled in the contentment, awareness flaring deep inside. Tension built with every passing moment. War loomed on the horizon—they'd already paid a steep cost in blood. But more was coming…and all he could do was brace for the oncoming storm.

* * *

Sometime between bouts of sex, they managed to find their way into bed and his phone vibrated twice in as many minutes.

"Don't you think you should answer that? It might be important." Sleep muddied Bethany's voice.

"If it's important they would have used the ear communication when I didn't answer the first time." Raja lay still, ignoring the phone.

Whoever called hung up and placed the call again. The cell phone near the end of the dresser teetered, about to fall off.

She yawned. "I don't think they'll give up."

He growled as he reached to grab it. Pressing the talk button, he snarled, "What?"

Connor needed to see him. He'd found something. *Dammit.* "Connor's on his way. He wants you to look at something. That boy has the worst timing." Irritated by the interruption, he also understood it. They were at war. Hadn't he just been appreciating those fleeting moments of passion and peace? He growled.

Raja dressed in jeans and armed himself. The battle hardened habits so ingrained he didn't have to think about it. In the bathroom, he splashed cold water on his face. The musk of their couplings still heavy in the air soothed the agitated tiger inside. Bethany followed in a pair of grey cotton lounge pants and a pink and grey tank top, beautiful, feminine...and utterly flimsy in their colder climate.

"You need more clothes. I know you only had a few things with you. Order whatever you'd like online and we'll have it shipped."

"I'm fine. I'm sure I can get someone to ship my things from Virginia." She pulled her hair into a ponytail.

"No, that won't be possible."

"What do you mean?"

"Most of the stuff inside the house was destroyed, particularly your things." He tried to keep his tone light, but it was just another sign of Pierce's madness. Destroying her home—her family—her things. He wanted to erase Bethany.

"Everything?" She locked gazes with him.

"Anything that could be salvaged, pictures, mementos, valuables, Jinx has a team there to gather them once the police are done with the scene. With clothes and things like that it would be best to get you new. If there is anything particular that you would like them to check for I can get them that information."

"Jamie had a music box that she loved. I'd like it. Mom's jewelry. After a fire when I was a kid, she kept it in fire-safe box under her bed. Pictures. There are photo albums that line the bookcase in the living room. Dad always loved taking pictures." She sank to the bed. "I thought I was coming to grips with this…"

"It will take time, love." He knelt in front of her. "It's hard to lose your parents no matter how old you are. Even worse to lose a sister. I remember the pain when my parents died. I bottled it up inside me. I couldn't grieve, not when I had my sister to care for and the clan. But eventually it happened, and it was worse than if I would have dealt with it when it happened. Don't put on a brave face for me. I love you no matter what. We'll get through this."

A knock interrupted and he sighed.

Bethany gave him a weak, watery smile, but beneath her ghost white expression he saw the strength in her. "Go and let Connor in.

Give me a minute and I'll be out. I want to wash my face and pull myself together."

"Don't be long. You need some sleep before you pass out on your feet." He kissed her. *She's strong. She'll get through this. No one can replace her family, but hopefully Tora and the clan can help ease her pain.*

He opened the door to find not only Connor, but Lukas as well. "Come in. Bethany will be out in a moment." He held the door wide, eyeing Lukas.

"After Jinx spoke with you and Ty, I offered my services to Connor. Computers have always been my passion, finding people is new to me. My skills lie in hacking." Lukas explained.

"He's brilliant when it comes to hacking. It's how we were able to find the information as quickly as we did." Connor followed behind, carrying a laptop and a folder with what looked like printed papers hanging out of it.

"If either of you ever betray us, we could be in serious danger," Raja shook his head, not seriously considering either of them would betray the clan. Connor might be a wolf-shifter, but he had found a place among the Alaskan Tigers, and Lukas's devotion to the tigers was pure.

"Never." They swore in unison.

"Then let's hope they don't have anyone as talented as you two on their side. Please have a seat."

"About that, I'm sorry to bother you at this unthinkable hour. But if we don't have the right people, it would be wasted time going after the wrong lead. A quick confirmation from her and we can be out of your hair." Connor looked at Raja nervously.

Connor had a rocky past with shifters, first from his own kind and then with Pierce, making his apprehension understandable. "No worries. We'd rather be disturbed than have you waste hours looking into the wrong people."

"Whatever I can do to help." A calmer Bethany entered the room. Raja held out his hand and she crossed to take her place at his side. The ease and the comfort he took in her presence was profound. He couldn't imagine a time when she hadn't been with him.

"I believe we might have found Robin. I have two pictures for you to look at. One is of Robert 'Bobby' Zimmer and the other is of Robin. I need to know if you believe there are the people you knew in school." Connor nodded to her.

"Okay. Bobby was a year ahead of me in school and we were acquaintances, if that."

"Did you know Robin?" Lukas asked, setting up the laptop.

"No. She was three or four years younger and was coming into the high school as I left. I never did understand how they became a couple, especially in high school. She was so young, a freshman in high school, while he was already in his second year of college."

"Bethany, that's Lukas. He's Jinx's younger brother. I'm sure you heard from either Tabitha or Tora. He's the tiger that appeared injured during Tabitha's homecoming party." Raja gently pulled Bethany toward the couch. Tiredness weighed heavily on her.

"It's nice to finally meet you." Bethany smiled.

"Here's what we could find." Connor turned the computer screen around and two pictures side by side were on the screen.

The woman looked no older than her late teens, early twenties if that. She had long black hair, and the terror in her eyes pained Raja. The man in the second picture looked older. His face was harsh and weathered as if he had lived a hard life. His eyes were cold, and a look of hatred filled his face.

"That's them. What happened to them? He was an attractive guy when I knew him. He liked to drink and party, but look at him. The hatred is apparent in his body language. She looks downright terrified."

"Like you said, he liked to drink. He cared more for the bottle than anything else. Seems he got himself into quite a bit of trouble with both the law and loan sharks. He's been in and out of jail for the last few years, until he ended up dead. From what we were able to find on the police reports, I believe Pierce ordered the hit."

"What about Robin?" Bethany asked, still looking at the picture.

"Her cousin filed a missing person report on her. According to the cousin, Robin was worried about someone that Bobby owned money to, and they were after her. That's all we found so far. It's possible Pierce and his gang have already found her." Connor turned the screen around, closing the laptop.

"No, he doesn't have her *yet*. He's after her. We need to find Robin first. Get us a lead; find out where she might have gone. Find any family she might have stayed with. In the meantime, get me what you have on the cousin. Check the financials, maybe the cousin gave her money so she could hind under the radar. Find me something." Raja ordered. They needed everything—they needed to catch a break. The tip about Victor was one, but the sooner they stopped Pierce the better for everyone involved.

"Yes, sir." Lukas and Connor grabbed their stuff.

"You think she's still alive?" Bethany asked Raja when they were alone.

"She has to be. The book wouldn't send us on this search if she wasn't. I believe once we find her, she'll be able to help us. If not then what's the point of this?"

"Maybe the point is to save her."

"We would have done it anyway. The book says she holds a key to finding Pierce. We need to find out who Pierce has in his pocket or as part of his clan before we can move forward in uniting the tigers. If we don't, it will only lead to more betrayal."

Chapter Thirty-Two

"Tora's on the line. She wants to know if they can bring anything." Raja held the phone toward her.

"Tell her just bring themselves." Bethany finished basting the chicken and slid the roaster back in the oven.

"You heard her. Don't forget my beautiful niece."

Tora cut him off. "Speaking of that. I'm going to have Daniella watch her. I want to get to know Bethany without having to watch Scarlet. Plus you know Scarlet goes to bed early. If I bring her she always wakes up on the way back to our cabin and its' so hard to get her back to sleep."

"Then bring Daniella along. She can take her back to your cabin for bed. I want to see my niece. James will be here as well tonight. See you soon." He hung up before his sister could give him another excuse to leave Scarlet at home.

"She didn't want to bring Scarlet?" Bethany peeled potatoes over the sink.

"Normally they put Scarlet to bed early when they have family dinners, as it allows the grownup time that she craves. She planned to leave Scarlet at home with Daniella. I hope you don't mind that Daniella will be coming as well. She'll be here to play with Scarlet and then take her home to bed."

"No, that's fine. If there is anyone else you want to invite, please feel free."

"No, I don't want any of them here. I want you all to myself." He came up behind her to wrap his arms around her and kiss her neck. "I have to admit I find this awful sexy."

"What, me in the kitchen? With flour on my shirt, my hair clipped back in this messy style to keep it off my neck because of the heat? This turns you on?"

"Umm-humm," he traced the whorls of her ear with his tongue.

"If I knew you were that easy to turn on, I wouldn't have gone to all this work," she teased.

"This isn't for my benefit. You're doing this to repay Tora. Can I distract you?" He might as well have been a teenage boy discovering sex for the first time.

"No. You'll have to wait. I'm going to put these potatoes on and then jump in the shower. Before you even ask, no, you can't join me. You need to watch dinner."

"You're taking all the fun out of this mating," he teased, nuzzling her neck.

"Tonight, I promise. Now go over to Tabitha's, because she's letting me borrow her cupcake rack. I was digging around in the cabinets trying to find something to display the cupcakes on when she stopped by earlier."

"You made cupcakes?"

"I make a delicious devil food cupcake with buttercream icing. I made them when you were discussing guard schedules with Shadow. I thought it would be a nice dessert after the roasted chicken, rosemary potatoes and vegetables." She seasoned the last of the potatoes before placing them in a baking dish and putting them in the oven. "Now, go get it so I can shower and get ready."

* * *

Bethany iced the last cupcake and placed it on the rack. She licked the spoon clean of the remaining icing and looked around the room. *Everything seems ready but I feel as if I'm forgetting something.* She left the cupcake rack on the kitchen bar and grabbed the dishes to set the table.

"Bethy." She turned to find her Uncle James.

"Uncle James, I'm glad you came."

"I wouldn't miss it. You look beautiful. What can I do?"

"Thanks. Everything's almost ready. Tora and Marcus should be along soon. Until then we are waiting. Can I get you something to drink? A beer? Coffee? Soda?"

"Have a beer with me, James." Raja came strolling into the kitchen freshly showered and dressed. His hair still damp from the shower hung loose, giving him an angelic look.

Wow. I thought he looked killer in jeans. It's nothing compared to how he fills out those dress slacks and pullover green sweater. Keeping my hands off him until everyone leaves might be a challenge. Wonder if anyone would notice if we slipped away? What am I saying—they would hear us.

"Sure, I'll have a beer."

"I'll get them," Raja told Bethany as she set down the plates and turned toward the refrigerator.

Her eyes followed him as she sat the table. *I want to run my hands over his body.* She took a deep breath, trying to push the lust from her thoughts. "You're having a beer?" She looked at him shocked he was drinking anything but coffee.

"Once in a while it's okay to enjoy a cold beer." He ran his hand down her arm and kissed her check as he walked past. "Tora texted while I was in the shower. She'll be here shortly. Scarlet spilled her apple juice down the front of her dress. Marcus is giving her a quick bath, to clean up the sticky mess I call my niece."

"Ahh, that must be her." Raja passed a beer to James and went to answer the door.

"I hope you won't be uncomfortable tonight," she whispered to her uncle as she neared him, placing the last plate at the end chair. It might have been years since they were together, but he was still her family. Her only living family.

"It's fine. They're part of your family now. Tora did a beautiful job on the service."

He's right—they're my family now. Then why am I so anxious? Deep breaths, you can do this.

"How's my Scarlet?" Raja took his niece from Tora, tossing her slightly in the air to make the toddler giggle.

"If you make her sick, Raja, you'll be cleaning it," His sister scolded.

"She loves it."

Bethany stood close to the kitchen counter, watching them. When Tora rolled her eyes, she couldn't help but laugh. "Thank you for coming."

"It's our pleasure. I wish you would have let me bring something. Can I do anything in the kitchen?"

"I told you she's used to being in control when it comes to family dinners."

"Thank you, Tora, but I have it covered. Everything's in the oven and should be ready in fifteen minutes. Until then please make yourself at home."

"Have a seat. Marcus, want a beer? Tora, that revolting root beer that you prefer?" Raja asked as Scarlet tugged on his hair. When they nodded, he placed Scarlet on the floor and headed to the kitchen. "Where's Daniella?"

"Tonight's the night for the monthly chat for her online college class. She'll be over after that to take Scarlet home. I brought her a few toys that should keep her occupied."

Bethany watched as Scarlet came toddling toward her. The pudgy little legs looking unsteady as she made her way across the room. When she came close, she tugged on Bethany's jeans with her little chubby fists.

"Seems as if she likes you." Tora laughed. "She wants you to lift her. She's our cuddling kitty."

Bethany leaned down and picked up Scarlet as if she was fine china.

"She won't break," Tora teased.

"I haven't been around children this young in a long time. Jamie was the last toddler I had any real contact with, she's...umm...was...seventeen." Scarlet wrapped her arms around Bethany's neck, bringing her closer, and gave her a slobbery kiss.

"You were always so caring with Jamie. You were like a little mother to her. You'll make a wonderful mother when your time comes." James leaned against the wall, drinking his beer and watching Bethany closely.

"She'll have you wrapped around her fingers before long. She's had Uncle Raja there since she was an infant." Tora unloaded the bag of toys she had, putting them on the living room floor for Scarlet to play with. "Look on the bright side—she's the perfect introduction to your own."

Chapter Thirty-Three

The table was cluttered with documents and pictures. Two different groups were working on different situations. Connor and Lukas sat at the far end, their eyes unblinking from the laptops in front of them. Behind them, there was a board with a map of the United States, with different colored pins poking out. Each pin represented a place Robin was seen and her trail zigzagging across the U.S.A. While at the other end of the conference table Marcus, Thomas, Shadow and Felix worked feverishly, trying to gather information on Victor and the Russian tiger that were set to meet in less than twenty-four hours.

Ty, Raja and Jinx sat in the middle of the conference table going over the information that had already accumulated. "I spoke with Adam this morning. Victor checked into the hotel. They're standing down to see if the Russian makes an appearance. No information has been found as to why they're meeting. Unless Victor flees they're going to observe," Raja said, tossing aside another folder.

"We've got less than twenty-four hours to find out whatever we can about this Russian. Otherwise, Adam and the team will have to take down Victor. Taking down Victor will upset the balance of Pierce's gang and hopefully make him think twice before any future attacks."

"Now this is interesting." Raja passed over a fresh folder to Ty. "It would seem as though Victor's mother is Russian. From the financials, it appears that he's receiving money quarterly from an account in Russia. Connor, can you trace the money, find out where it's coming from?"

"If there's another laptop around here, I can start the process to narrow it down as I continue with Robin's trail. When it's finished narrowing down the points of origin, I'll give Lukas what I have on Robin and attend to that." Connor didn't look up from the laptop. "I don't mean to sound demanding, but if we could set up a computer station. I'd be able to run multiple searches simultaneously."

"Start the search. Then find whatever you need online and order it. Rush the shipping if you have to. We'll turn one of the smaller conference rooms into what you need." Ty scanned the papers Raja handed him. "Felix, I have an extra laptop in the top drawer of my desk. Would you please get it? I also want you to find out whatever you can on Victor's mother. Who's his father? Siblings? Who was Victor before he became Pierce's right-hand man?"

"It will take some time to find what you've requested."

"Unfortunately time is one thing we don't have. Lukas, can you handle tracking Robin's course?"

"Sure. Right now we are a few months behind her." Lukas stabbed another colored pin into the map then grabbed a marker to put the date she was seen there.

"Good. Connor, focus on Victor, see what you can find, and quickly. I know you both are working around the clock, and we appreciate it. No one else here has the computer expertise that you two do. Maybe we can recruit or train others to help you in the future but, as of right now, this is a need to know only situation." Felix returned with the laptop, handing it to Connor as Ty spoke. "Ahh, here you go. When you find something let us know. In the meantime, Raja and I have some other things we need to attend to. Shadow, Felix with us. The rest of you keep working."

* * *

Bethany and Tabitha were in Ty's quarters hunkered down in front of Ty's laptop, shopping, with Styx standing guard.

"Are you two spending all our money?" Ty teased, gracefully taking a seat on the opposite couch. "We were gone for over two hours, and you're still shopping?"

"Women can spend a day shopping. You make our task harder having to do it online. We can't see how it will look on us, or how it feels," Tabitha told him before pointing to something on the screen. "This would look great on you, Bethany."

"I can't believe you're the same woman I took shopping in Pennsylvania who barely bought anything."

"That was different. First because I had a target on my back and I wanted to get out of town. Second because it's more fun to shop

217

with another woman. I'm just giving my expert opinion on what would look good on her."

"So you're not buying then?" Ty questioned.

"I didn't say that."

"We left our women with our credit cards; did you really expect to find them finished shopping?" Raja leaned against the arm of the couch. "I know you both prefer jeans and sweaters. Nevertheless, make sure you order a couple dressy outfits. It's possible you will need them as things progress."

"See and I told you this would look great on you."

"Okay, but that's it. I bought enough clothes," Bethany said, adding the dress to her shopping cart.

"You don't get off that easy. You need shoes to go with these and the other outfits."

"While the women finish their shopping spree, why don't we take this to my office?" Ty rose and stretched before strolling toward his office.

Inside the office, Raja grabbed four water bottles from the micro-fridge, handing them to Shadow, Felix, Ty and keeping one for himself. "What's up, Ty?"

"Once Adam and the team detain Victor, we're going to need a place to take him. Raja and I decided we don't want him here at the compound. Remember Taber, the Kodiak bear shifter from Nome? His family has a few cabins about an hour's drive from here, less in the helicopter. I've already contacted him, and he agreed to meet us there." Ty took a sip of water before setting it on his desk, and plopping down in the office chair.

"Are you suggesting taking your mates?" Felix sat in front of Ty's desk, water bottle untouched in his hands.

"It's something Ty and I have gone back and forth on. Pierce knows the location of the compound, making it more dangerous here. In addition we would have to leave some of the key people behind to protect our mates. Whereas if they were with us, kept safely in a farther cabin we would still be able to protect them while having the key group together to interrogate Victor." Raja set the half drank bottle of water aside. He didn't want it. Instead he wanted coffee. Soon, he promised himself.

"But there would be no perimeter set up. No guards on guard duty."

"Good point, Felix. I'm sure Taber could bring a couple of his family members to patrol the grounds, or…" Raja's attention was diverted from Felix when Shadow let out a soft moan, grabbing her temple. "Shadow? What is it?" Raja stood quickly, catching her as her knees buckled.

"Ahh," she moaned at Raja gently placed her on the chair he vacated.

"Should we get the doctor?"

"No. I just need a moment." She let her eyes close while everyone else stood around watching her. "No cabin. More dangerous."

"Are you sure, Shadow?" Raja kneeled in front of her.

"Yes. Someone that Taber knows, I'm not sure who, owes Pierce a favor. He'll squeal that something is going on at the cabins…there will be an attack if you go there. Have Taber come here without telling anyone. The cabin on the edge of the compound. It needs work but it would do for this. Put Victor there."

"Having him here might raise the chance for attack." Ty looked out the window. "It puts more lives on the line. Not only the guards but mates, women and children."

"It does, but there are more guards here to protect everyone. We'll raise the security level and keep everyone on call. It's the best chance to keep everyone safe if Shadow's vision is true. Splitting our guards between two places will make us weaker."

"Okay, Felix, Shadow I want you to take the guest rooms. I want you in the main building with us. Even with other guards on our mates, I want you within seconds away from them. If there's an attack, I want the women guarded together if it's safe enough to move one of them. This will allow for more guards on them." Ty closed the curtain before facing them again. "Tabitha and Bethany's training starts tonight. I want them well versed in shooting a gun. I have started Tabitha's hand to hand training but if there's an attack, their best chance is weapons that allow them to keep their distances."

"Give us about an hour to debrief the others then meet us back here to go to the firing range." Raja rose from his kneeling position in front of Shadow but still eyed her cautiously. "Are you okay now?"

"I'm fine." Shadow stood and followed Felix out, leaving Raja and Ty alone.

"I'll let you have the honor of telling Tabitha and Bethany. After all, you're Alpha here." Raja winked.

Marissa Dobson

Chapter Thirty-Four

The shooting range turned out better than Raja could ever expect. Bethany's father had already taught her how to shoot a gun, and she proved to be a decent shot. Tabitha wasn't too bad either for someone who only held a gun once before, and that was only since becoming Ty's mate.

"You've both done very well. I want you both to keep the guns with you. If you want shoulder and thigh holsters, we can get them for you. Even with your guards, I want you armed in case something happens. Once Victor arrives, Pierce might decide to attack." Raja grabbed a box of bullets off the shelf.

"Raja, Connor found something. He's requesting that you join them in the conference room." Felix informed him.

"I'll tend to it. Bethany, go with Ty, Tabitha and the guards. I'll come for you at Ty's when I can." He slid his reloaded gun back into his holster, kissed Bethany and jogged toward the main compound.

Please let this be a break we need. I hate feeling Bethany's panic. Tabitha and Bethany have been through enough recently—they don't need more stress.

After pulling the conference room door open, he found the room full of anxiety and all eyes trained on him. "What's going on?"

"We can't let the meeting Victor has scheduled happen," Connor announced, plugging the projector into the computer to allow whatever was on the screen to appear on the wall.

"Why? What did you find?"

"The man is Victor's father. He heads a small terrorist group of shifters in Russia. That's where the money is coming from. From what I can find this meeting is to discuss joining their forces, making both of them more treacherous than before." Connor displayed a table with numbers on the wall. "This tracks each transition back to the organization Victor's father heads. Victor Senior arrives tomorrow evening. My suggestion would be to have the team take down Victor tonight and get them out of San Francisco."

"Great job. I'll deal with Adam and the team. Marcus, gather any guard not on duty in the ballroom. Meeting in thirty minutes. Either Ty or I will brief everyone. Anyone on duty will be notified following the briefing. From this moment on everyone is on high alert and on call at all times. Thomas, you help him. Connor and Lukas, I want you both working on Robin, as I'm concerned this will put her in more jeopardy."

* * *

Raja spent the next fifteen minutes filling in Ty, Felix, Shadow and Styx on what Connor found. "Adam and the team need to take

Victor down tonight. We can't leave this to chance any longer. If Victor Senior gets there before he's detained, it could mean a full-on assault."

"I agree. Contact Adam and I'll brief the guards." Ty turned to the women. "You'll stay here with guards."

"Ty, with Victor soon to be on the grounds. I'd like Tora's family to take the final guest room here in the main building. If Marcus is called away, it leaves Tora and Scarlet easy targets."

"Agreed. Deal with Adam then see to Tora. Inform her that if there's an attack on the compound, she should find Tabitha and Bethany if it's safe to move within the main building. She'll be safe with them," Ty had his hand on the door handle when he turned around to face Raja who already had his cell phone out and dialing Adam's number. "Tell Adam in the medical kit Doc sent him with there a strong muscle relaxer that's used on our kind. I want Victor sedated for transport."

Raja nodded, hitting the call button. "Are you somewhere private?" he asked Adam as his voice filled the line.

"Good. The Russian is his father, Victor Senior. He heads a shifter terrorist group in Russia. Victor needs to be detained tonight. We want him sedated and brought bound and blindfolded back to the compound. Do you need more men?" *I pray not. There might not be enough time to get more men there.* "Great. Contact me when the job's done. Stay safe."

He hit the end button before clipping the phone back on his jeans. "I need to go see to Tora."

* * *

Bethany watched Raja leave and closed her eyes. *What the hell was I thinking to get involved in all of this? All I wanted was a quiet life.*

"Bethany, you okay?" Tabitha laid her hand on her leg.

"Okay? No, I'm not okay." Tears filled her eyes. "How do you deal with this?"

"With our men running off? The guards? The danger?"

"All of it. Don't you worry about, Ty? Aren't you scared that you're going to be the next to die?" Bethany snapped the ponytail holder off her wrist and pulled her hair back in a messy ponytail, to get it out of her face.

"I always worry about Ty, as well as Raja and the rest of the clan members. I don't want to see anyone else die because of this. Pierce has taken too many lives as it is. I deal by realizing that it has to be done. If not Pierce is out there with a free killing pass. I can't live with that. I'll do whatever I can to see him pay for what happened to our parents, Jamie, and countless other victims. There's danger but there's danger everywhere. You could walk outside and a bus hits you. I'd rather live my life to the fullest with the man I love than cower in fear."

"But we are cowering behind the guards."

"I don't see it as cowering. We have a job to do for the tigers. We have to be kept safe until the job is complete." She sounded utterly reasonable.

"That might be fine enough for you. You're their Queen. Me, on the other hand, I'm no one." Bethany leaned her head back, resting it on the back of the couch.

"That's where you're wrong, Bethany. Without you we could never do what the future holds for us." Tabitha gave her an encouraging smile.

"What?"

"After I came back to the clan, the book you've already seen told us that Raja had to find his mate before we could start the process of bringing the tigers together. You're part of this destiny as much as the rest of us. You'll play a key point in this. Don't doubt that you're meant to be here or that Raja would give his life for you." Tabitha squeezed her leg.

"That's the problem. I don't want him to give his life for me. I don't want to live without him."

Shadow walked from the window, coming around the couch to squat near Bethany. "I'm sure Raja has told you of my gift. That I know things, mates, the future, pasts. I can tell you there's nothing to worry about. Nothing is going to happen to Raja. You'll be together for many years. One way to protect your mates, don't fight them on your guards. They want to keep you safe. You are their top priority, but they also have other things they must worry about. If they know you'll listen to your guards and we'll keep you safe, it will allow them to focus on whatever task is at hand."

* * *

As expected Tora fought Raja—she didn't want to leave her cabin, until Marcus returned from the briefing and put his foot down. "I agree with Raja that it's a precaution that we should take. Now go pack what you need for yourself and Scarlet. You have twenty minutes. I won't have you and Scarlet alone as a target when I'm needed to defend the compound. At least in the main building you'll be safe. There will be more guards there."

After Tora stormed out of the room, leaving them alone, Marcus turned to Raja. "Taber will be landing in ten minutes. Ty's meeting him at the landing field. I'm sure you would rather be there. Also Adam's team will move in on Victor within the hour."

"Appreciated. Get her moving. I want her in the main building long before Victor is detained."

After leaving Tora's cabin, he pulled out his cell phone to text Shadow. *Moving to the landing strip. Taber's due in. Adam moves on Victor within the hour.*

Chapter Thirty-Five

"Taber, this is my mate Bethany and Ty's mate Tabitha. Ladies, Taber is a Kodiak bear shifter. He's been generous enough to come look intimidating while we interrogate Victor."

"Wow," Tabitha and Bethany both quietly whispered.

"I know my size can be daunting, but I promise you unless provoked, I'm a big teddy bear. Ty, Raja and I go back many years. I'm only here to help." Taber stood almost seven-foot-three; every part of his body was toned and tight. His massive frame made people shy away at first glance but not Tabitha and Bethany—they stared at him with open mouths.

"I'm sorry." Bethany blinked a few times. She looked as if she wanted to pinch herself to make sure she was truly awake. "I just never..."

"Don't worry, Bethany, I get that reaction a lot."

"I didn't mean to be impolite."

"I understand. Raja tells me shifters are new to you. I hope you won't hold my size against me."

"I should apologize as well," Tabitha said, shaking her head like a cat would to shed water.

"Now that we have the stares and apologies out of the way, maybe we can move on." Raja laughed, amused by their reaction. "Bethany, Taber is going to bunk in our guest room since the main guest accommodations are full. I hope you don't mind."

"No, that's fine. I hope you'll find it suitable."

"Where's Ty?" Tabitha looked to the door as if expecting him to be only moments behind Raja and Taber.

"He went with Milo and Thomas to check on the cabin we'll be using. He'll be back shortly. When he gets back, we're going to have some downtime. Anyone who wants to catch some sleep before shit hits the fan better do it. Adam's team is taking down Victor within the hour. If all goes well within the next six hours, they should be here." Fatigue began to make itself known to Raja as he dropped to the couch like a ton of bricks. Too much stress, long hours and not enough sleep finally started to catch up to him.

"You want some coffee?" Tabitha asked.

"No thanks." He rubbed his eyes with his thumb and forefinger before squeezing the bridge of his nose. "I'm going to try to catch a few winks once Ty's back. Tabitha, while Ty and I are questioning Victor, Felix and Thomas will be guarding you. Shadow and Styx will be with you, Bethany. If anything changes, the guards will bring Bethany here, unless this area is compromised. We decided this since Ty's quarters overlook the main area of the compound, giving the guards a chance to see out, and because it's more protected. Marcus will remain with Tora unless he's needed. They're just down the hall in one of the guest rooms."

He went over the strategy while they waited for Ty. They agreed to keep the women and the guards abreast on the situations. Being informed allowed them to be ready if and when something happened.

Raja's cell vibrated as he looked up to see Ty and Thomas entering. *Moving on him. Will contact once he's in custody.*

* * *

Raja lay on top of the covers next to Bethany, dozing. She slept deeply, but even in sleep she held onto him. He could feel her uneasiness and knew she was fearful of losing him. She'd lost so much already and was scared she would lose him as she'd lost the rest of her family.

How am I supposed to alleviate her concerns when anything could happen? I've never been naive enough to think I didn't put my life on the line. It's my job to put myself after the members of the clan and to protect Ty and Tabitha at all cost. Having a mate frightened because of my position is the reason I avoided mating. Oh Bethany, I wish I could take your fears away, to promise I'll always be here for you.

He brushed a stray hair away from her face, when his phone vibrated.

He's in custody. Little worse for wear, but he'll live. Boarding plane now.

The news he had been waiting for. *Call when you're an hour out. Great job.*

Team's on the way with Victor. They'll call an hour out. He quickly typed the message to Ty before closing his eyes again.

"I thought you were supposed to be sleeping?" She peered at him through half-mast eyes.

"The phone woke me," he lied.

"About Victor?"

"They're on their way." He nodded. "Should be here in roughly six hours."

* * *

They couldn't have timed Victor's arrival better if they tried. It was the early morning hours. The compound was quiet and only the guards patrolling the grounds. They doubled the number of guards on each shift, as well as adding extra guards to guard Victor. A makeshift cell was installed in the cabin, allowing them to hold Victor without concerns.

The lights lined the runway as all eyes turned to the plane coming into view. Ty and Raja stood surrounded by a few chosen guards, and the air around them sizzled with their energy. They were anxious to deal with Victor, but knew the hopes of finding out something useful about Pierce were doubtful. If Victor had any honor or loyalty, he wouldn't betray Pierce.

"If he is badly injured, Galen should be here," Doc said, coming to stand next to Raja.

"You're not here to heal him, unless he is dying. You're here only to make sure his wounds won't kill him before we have a chance to question him. If he's suffering from injuries from his attempt to avoid capture, then so be it. He deserves them."

The plane landed before Doc could argue further, but he had no doubt he would hear Doc's complaints in time. "Let's break this bastard," Raja announced, jogging toward the plane that stopped a few yards in front of them.

Raja's life was fuller than he ever expected. He found his mate, and Bethany somehow changed his heart. She went through hell, but came out stronger. She lost everything yet remained willing to love again. She gave him back his reason for living.

He was no longer just the Lieutenant of the Alaskan Tiger's; no he was also her mate. With more determination to keep his mate and the clan safer than ever, he opened the plane door, and dragged out the drugged Victor. Anger invigorated him, Victor, Pierce and their rogue gang hunted he and his kind, but Raja would not stop until he dismantled them all—for Ty, for Tabitha, and Bethany.

"Time to play Victor. I have a war to win."

The war is on...

ABOUT THE AUTHOR

Born and raised in the Pittsburgh, Pennsylvania area, Marissa Dobson now resides about an hour from Washington, D.C. She's a lady who likes to keep busy, and is always busy doing something. With two different college degrees, she believes you're never done learning.

Being the first daughter to an avid reader, this gave her the advantage of learning to read at a young age. Since learning to read she has always had her nose in a book. It wasn't until she was a teenager that she started writing down the stories she came up with.

Marissa is blessed with a wonderful supportive husband, Thomas. He's her other half and allows her to stay home and pursue her writing. He puts up with all her quirks and listens to her brainstorm in the middle of the night.

Her writing buddies Max (a cocker spaniel) and Dawne (a beagle mix) are always around to listen to her bounce ideas off them. They might not be able to answer, but they're helpful in their own ways.

She love to hear from readers so send her an email at marissa@marissadobson.com or visit her website www.marissadobson.com

Other Books by Marissa Dobson

Tiger Time

Storm Queen

Snowy Fate

Sarah's Fate

Mason's Fate

As Fate Would Have It

Learning to Live

Learning What Love Is

Her Cowboy's Heart

Passing On

Restoring Love

Winterbloom

Secret Valentine

The Twelve Seductive Days of Christmas

CPSIA information can be obtained at www.ICGtesting.com
Printed in the USA
LVOW11s1959160614

390268LV00001B/382/P